LOVE IN THE LATER INNINGS

Vivian Hartwell

CONTENTS

CHAPTER ONE

March 2003, Phoenix, Arizona

The evening air was warm, the desert heat from the day still radiating off the metal bleachers as Maggie Callahan settled into her seat. The sky was dusky purple, streaked with the last threads of orange, and the scent of grilled hot dogs and stale mingled in the air. "This is nice," Brenda sighed, stretching out in the fold-down stadium chair. "I don't know why we don't do this more often."

"Because none of us are baseball fans," Lynn pointed out, tipping her sunglasses down to give Brenda a look.

Maggie smiled but didn't contribute to the debate.

She hadn't been to a baseball game in years. Decades, maybe. She'd watched a few innings here and there when it was on at a bar, when the World Series was in full swing, but it wasn't something she followed.

Not anymore.

She used to love it once.

Or maybe, she used to love someone who loved it.

But that was a lifetime ago.

"This is minor league, right?" Debbie asked, squinting at the field.

"No," Brenda laughed. "Spring Training—real MLB players

warming up. It doesn't count for anything."

Debbie frowned. "So, what's the point?"

"To drink beer outside in seventy-degree weather and stare at men in tight pants."

A ripple of laughter went through their little group, and Maggie chuckled along with them, taking a slow sip of her beer.

The truth was, she wasn't sure why she'd agreed to come tonight.

Girls' nights out weren't really her thing—not anymore. She wasn't against them, but since she retired last year, she felt a little adrift. Like she was supposed to be enjoying all this free time but couldn't figure out what to do with it. She'd started in '62, fresh from Vandy, typing memos for some Memphis firm—40 years later, she ended up in Phoenix been running HR for half the Southwest.

Maybe she just didn't want to sit alone in her house.

The game had already started—the bottom of the third inning, apparently. She wasn't really following, just letting the hum of the crowd and the easy conversation of her friends wash over her. She stretched her legs out, crossed her ankles, and let her gaze drift across the field. A batter adjusted his gloves in the box, the catcher crouched behind the plate, and the pitcher stood, glove pressed to his chest, eyes locked on the catcher's signal. Her gaze slid past them, toward the dugouts. Then to third base. Where the coach stood, signaling toward the runner. Maggie's breath caught. She wasn't sure what, exactly, made her stop. Maybe it was his posture.

Maybe it was the way he tilted his head, hands on his hips, waiting. Something about him felt familiar. A long-buried instinct pricked the back of her mind. Her eyes flicked to the back of his jersey.

RIGGS.

Her stomach dropped. Riggs—a common name, a coincidence. Yet as the third-base coach turned, calling to the batter under the stadium lights, her grip tightened on her beer cup. No way. But her heart hammered. But now that she truly saw him, recognition was undeniable. It was impossible not to recognize him. Jack Riggs. Her Jack. Or, at least, the man he had become. His face was older, sharper. His once-boyish cockiness had settled into something leaner, wearier. His hair was mostly silver now, but still thick. His broad shoulders still held that effortless athlete's stance. Thirty years disappeared in an instant. Maggie was twenty again, standing in the stands of a minor-league stadium, watching him take the field. She had thought she'd put all of this behind her. But here he was. Alive. Real. Less than a hundred feet away. And he had no idea she was watching. Her stomach twisted. She hadn't seen him since 1961. Since that game in Nashville, when she had hoped —prayed—he'd notice her. That night had been the final straw. She had waited, waited, and finally walked away. Now, all these years later, she was waiting again. But this time, she wasn't that young girl, hoping for a sign. She was a sixty-three-year-old woman. And Jack Riggs was nothing more than a man in a baseball uniform. So why couldn't she look away?

CHAPTER TWO

A few nights later, Maggie found herself at a restaurant she wouldn't have chosen. It restaurant was dimly lit, with a lengthy wine list and the warm aroma of seared steak and buttered asparagus in the air. Maggie liked it well enough. It was nice, and nice was all she wanted tonight.

"You should try the cabernet," Brenda said, swirling her own glass. "I think it's better than the merlot."

Maggie glanced at her nearly full glass and smirked. "I'll keep that in mind when I finish this one. Which, at the rate this conversation is going, might be soon."

Brenda laughed, nudging her husband, Mark, who was busy scanning the bourbon selection. "She's impossible, isn't she?"

"She's drinking. That's progress," Mark offered dryly. He glanced at Maggie. "That means you're at least tolerating the date."

Maggie didn't answer right away. Tolerating was about right.

Her date—Rob? Ron—was in the restroom, and she wasn't exactly counting the seconds until he returned. A retired real estate developer who spoke as if still closing million-dollar deals, Ron had dominated dinner, expounding on Scottsdale's booming housing market and the steal of his golf course condo. Initially, Maggie had nodded politely, sipping her wine, waiting for him to ask about her. He never did.

That wasn't entirely surprising.

She'd been on enough of these "why not" dates over the years to know how this went. Some men, particularly successful men, had spent so much time talking about themselves that they assumed everyone else found them fascinating. Ron filled the silence effortlessly—provided it was about him. He wasn't rude. He wasn't arrogant, exactly. He was just... unaware.

And Maggie was very aware of how little she cared about Scottsdale's housing market.

Brenda must have sensed it, because she leaned in, dropping her voice. "Okay, honest opinion. He's not your type, is he?"

Maggie smiled, amused. "I didn't realize I had a type."

Brenda scoffed, exchanging a glance with Mark. "Oh, come on."

Maggie lifted a brow. "What?"

"You had a type," Brenda said knowingly, her voice teasing. "Back in the day."

Mark smirked but wisely said nothing.

Maggie rolled her eyes. "That was a long time ago."

"Doesn't mean it wasn't true." Brenda tipped her wine glass toward her. "Athletes. You had a thing for them."

Maggie's grip tightened around the stem of her glass, but her expression didn't waver.

"It wasn't a thing," she said lightly. "I just... dated one. Once."

Brenda's eyes glimmered with amusement. "One?"

"Okay, maybe two," Maggie admitted. "But that's not a type. It was... circumstantial."

Brenda grinned like she'd won something. "Athletes. Definitely a type."

Maggie shook her head. "I wouldn't go that far."

"Oh, I would." Brenda settled back in her seat, swirling her wine. "It makes sense, though. You've always liked men who were driven. Who had that… confidence."

Maggie opened her mouth to argue, then closed it.

Because Brenda wasn't wrong.

There was a time in her life when she had been drawn to that particular kind of energy—the kind that belonged to men who moved fast and reached high. Men who had big dreams and didn't look back.

Men who, more often than not, left people behind.

She glanced at the empty chair across from her, the one Ron would be returning to any second now, and something in her chest tightened.

Brenda sighed dramatically, nudging Mark. "She's impossible."

Mark chuckled, shaking his head. "Give it up, Bren. If Maggie wanted to date, she'd date."

"She is dating." Brenda gestured to the empty chair. "She's on a date right now."

Mark smirked. "A pity date isn't the same thing."

Maggie laughed, shaking her head. "I can hear you both, you know."

Brenda sighed again, but before she could respond, Ron returned, sliding back into his seat with an easy smile.

"Sorry about that," he said. "I ran into an old buddy in the lobby. Another guy who made a killing in commercial real estate before everything went corporate."

Maggie nodded absently, lifting her wine glass.

Ron took that as an invitation to continue.

"Anyway, as I was saying before, the real estate bubble is only just starting," he said. "Prices are gonna skyrocket in another five years. I mean, I'm glad I got in early, but if I were still in the game..." He shook his head, smiling to himself.

Maggie let Ron's words fade, no longer pretending to listen. She reached for the bread basket, tearing off a piece, her gaze drifting restlessly around the restaurant—past the clinking glasses, the shadowed booths—to a table near the bar. Her breath caught. Three men sat there, polo shirts and sport jackets exuding a familiar ease, but one of them - her chest tightened.

He was older, leaner than he'd been back then. The years had settled into him, sharpening the lines of his face, silver now streaked through his hair.

Jack Riggs.

He was sitting less than twenty feet away.

Maggie froze, her grip tightening on her wine glass. Twice in one week—meaningful, or just chance? She didn't linger on him, but she felt his presence.

And then, as if pulled by some invisible thread, Jack turned.

Their eyes met.

A second.

Two.

Three.

The air between them thickened.

Then—just like that—Jack looked away.

Maggie forced herself to breathe.

He wasn't going to come over.

And she wasn't going to get up.

And maybe that was fine.

Maybe that was for the best.

"Everything okay?" Brenda asked, her tone shifting just slightly, a quiet note of curiosity in it.

Maggie swallowed, shook her head lightly. "Yeah. Just thought I recognized someone."

Brenda glanced toward the bar, but Maggie took another sip of wine before she could ask anything else.

Ron, oblivious, kept talking.

"...if you know the right people, you can still make a fortune." He chuckled, shaking his head. "I always tell people, it's not about timing. It's about who you know."

Maggie barely heard him.

A moment later, she lifted her wine glass and did not look toward the bar again.

CHAPTER THREE

Maggie adjusted the strap of her clutch and stepped inside the ballroom, her eyes briefly sweeping across the crowd. The space was elegant—warm golden lighting, crisp white tablecloths, and the subtle clinking of glasses as servers wove between guests, refilling champagne flutes.

It had been a while since she'd attended something like this, but everything about it was familiar. The polished small talk, the hushed tones of people who wanted to appear important but not *too* eager.

She wasn't even sure why she'd agreed to come.

Except she knew exactly why.

Her former company had been involved in this charity for years, and when her old boss had called, inviting her to take a seat at their corporate table, she'd hesitated before saying yes. Retirement had given her plenty of excuses to say no to things, but lately, she was trying not to let herself sink too far into that habit.

Besides, it was a good cause.

And Jack Riggs being here had nothing to do with it.

She hadn't even known he'd be here.

At least, that's what she told herself as she made her way toward her assigned table, offering polite smiles to the few people she recognized from her years in corporate life.

"Ah, Maggie!" Richard Monroe, her former CEO, beamed as he stood to greet her. "I'm glad you could make it."

"Wouldn't miss it," she said, shaking his hand.

"The least I could do for our most legendary HR director," he teased, pulling out a chair for her. "Retirement treating you well?"

Maggie forced a smile as she sat. "So far."

She didn't mean to be vague, but the truth was, she hadn't quite figured out what *so far* even meant.

The seat beside her was empty, which she took as a small triumph, relieved she wouldn't have to spend the night stuck between a chatty executive and an overly enthusiastic date she didn't want.

A waiter appeared, pouring her a glass of wine, and she let herself relax.

Then—

The microphone crackled as the auctioneer took the stage.

"Alright, folks! We've got some amazing items up for bid tonight. Signed jerseys, private meet-and-greets, game-day experiences—"

Maggie took a slow sip of wine, only half-listening as he rattled off the lineup.

Until—

"And for all you baseball lovers out there, we've got a special experience donated by one of our very own tonight. A private hitting lesson with longtime MLB player and current Atlanta Braves coach, Jack Riggs!"

The name hit like a fastball to the ribs.

Maggie's fingers tightened around the stem of her glass.

Applause rippled through the crowd as Jack stepped onto the small stage, looking as at ease as ever.

He was dressed in a navy suit, but he still carried himself like an athlete—broad shoulders, the casual confidence of someone who spent decades being watched.

What were the odds?

Twice in one week at random could be shrugged off.

Three times?

That felt like something else entirely.

CHAPTER FOUR

Jack adjusted the microphone as the auctioneer grinned beside him.

"Anything you want to say about your donation tonight, Coach?"

He leaned slightly toward the mic, a small, easy smirk forming.

"Well, I can't promise to fix anyone's swing, but I can at least teach you how to look like you know what you're doing."

Laughter rippled through the room, light and genuine.

Jack relaxed slightly. He'd done plenty of these events over the years—charity auctions, fundraisers, youth baseball clinics. He liked them well enough. Giving back was part of the game. Helping kids get access to baseball felt like the right thing to do, and it sure as hell beat sitting through a corporate golf event where everyone just wanted to talk about his playing days.

The auctioneer clapped him on the back, launching into the opening bid.

Jack let his gaze wander over the audience as the numbers ticked higher.

And then—

His breath hitched.

Maggie.

His Maggie.

For a second, his mind short-circuited.

She was sitting at a table near the front, holding a glass of wine, her expression unreadable.

His fingers tensed slightly at his sides.

Running into her once had been unexpected.

Twice?

That felt like the past wasn't quite done with him yet.

The auctioneer's voice rose as the bids climbed higher, but Jack barely registered it.

Maggie wasn't looking at him anymore, and for some reason, that bothered him.

The auction wrapped. Someone won. Jack shook the guy's hand.

And then, without fully deciding to, he made his way off the stage, weaving through the crowd with purpose.

Toward her.

CHAPTER FIVE

Maggie saw him coming before he spoke.

She could feel it.

That familiar pull in her chest, the one she had spent decades convincing herself was long gone.

Jack stopped at her table, his hands tucked casually into his pockets, but there was something guarded about the way he stood.

"Maggie."

His voice was quieter than she remembered, but it still carried that same smooth, deliberate tone.

She looked up, meeting his eyes. "Jack."

A flicker of something passed through his expression—maybe relief that she'd said his name.

"Didn't expect to see you here," he said.

"Likewise." She swirled the wine in her glass. "I didn't realize the Braves were so involved in charity work."

Jack huffed a small laugh. "Yeah, well. Can't play forever. Gotta make yourself useful somehow."

She tapped the base of her wine glass against the table, considering him. "So, you're still in it."

"Yeah. Still in it."

She let that sit between them for a moment.

Baseball had always been his world. Back then, there had been no room for anything else.

And yet, here he was.

Still in it.

"You?" Jack asked, shifting his stance slightly. "Didn't see you as the retiring type."

Maggie lifted a shoulder. "It was time."

Jack studied her, his gaze steady but unreadable. "And you don't miss it?"

She took a sip of her wine, rolling the question over in her mind. Did she?

"I miss being useful," she admitted. "But I don't miss the late nights, the stress, the putting out fires all the time."

Jack smirked. "Sounds like coaching."

Maggie let out a small laugh. "Yeah, well. Maybe I should've gone into baseball."

"Could've used someone smart in the front office," he said, and she wasn't sure if it was a throwaway comment or something real.

She let her gaze drift over him again, noting the way he held himself. Still an athlete, but different now.

Different than she remembered.

Or maybe she just didn't know him anymore.

Jack shifted slightly, glancing at the glass in her hand. "So, what brought you here? You a baseball fan now?"

Maggie's lips parted, a retort forming, but before she could answer, Richard Monroe reappeared at the table.

"Maggie," Richard boomed, clapping her on the shoulder.

Jack resisted the urge to tense.

Richard was exactly the kind of guy who always seemed to be talking too loudly, taking up too much space.

"We're heading over to the silent auction—" Richard stopped, blinking at Jack. "Wait a minute. You're—"

Jack gave him a polite nod. "Jack Riggs."

Richard lit up. "Hell of a career. Didn't realize you were with the Braves now."

Jack gave a noncommittal shrug. "Been here a while."

Richard turned to Maggie, eyes gleaming. "Now, this is interesting. You two know each other?"

Maggie opened her mouth, not entirely sure how to answer that.

Jack beat her to it.

"College," he said smoothly, flicking her a glance. "Vanderbilt."

Richard's eyebrows lifted. "No kidding?" He laughed, shaking his head. "Small world."

Jack met Maggie's eyes again.

Yeah. Small world.

Richard Monroe's booming voice still echoed in Jack's ears as he strode off toward the silent auction, leaving him alone with Maggie again.

The interruption had done its job—it had punctured something, left the air different between them.

Jack seemed to reset himself, rolling his shoulders slightly. "You ever notice how people always love pointing out how small the world is?"

Maggie let out a quiet laugh, swirling the last bit of wine in her glass. "Maybe it's just small for some people."

Jack glanced around the room. "Or maybe it's just baseball. Feels like you never really leave it, even when you try."

She wasn't sure if he was talking about himself or her.

Maggie lifted her chin slightly, taking in the space around them. The ballroom had filled with movement—people drifting between tables, waiters maneuvering through the crowd with fresh trays of drinks, the faint murmur of bidding over at the auction area.

Jack hadn't walked away yet.

And neither had she.

"Come on," he said suddenly, tilting his head toward the back of the room. "Let's get out of the traffic."

Maggie hesitated, but only for a moment.

Jack wasn't asking her to go anywhere dramatic. Just somewhere a little quieter. Somewhere they could talk without Richard Monroe or the murmuring crowd around them.

She followed him past the last row of tables and toward a side hallway, where the hotel bar opened up into a lounge area. It was quieter here—still within earshot of the event but separate enough that it didn't feel like they were on display.

Jack leaned against the edge of the bar, hands still in his pockets. "So."

Maggie quirked a brow. "So?"

One corner of his mouth lifted. "You still haven't answered my question."

She tilted her head slightly, pretending not to know what he was referring to. "Which question was that?"

Jack gave her a look. "Are you a baseball fan now?"

Maggie huffed a quiet laugh, setting her empty wine glass on the bar. "I was never much of a fan. Not really."

Jack smirked. "Could've fooled me back then."

Something flickered between them.

A memory.

A life.

Maggie felt it hovering there, waiting for one of them to acknowledge it out loud.

She could still picture it—the summer heat pressing against her skin, the faded metal bleachers, the sharp crack of the bat as Jack sent a ball soaring into the outfield.

"I wasn't in it for the game," she said finally, meeting his gaze.

Jack held it. "I know."

Silence stretched between them, not uncomfortable, but thick. It felt strange to be here like this—two people with a history neither of them had figured out how to carry. Jack shifted slightly, exhaling.

"You look good, Mags."

The old nickname landed softly between them, familiar but foreign at the same time. Maggie's chest tightened. "I go by Maggie now." Jack nodded once, something unreadable flickering across his face. "Right. Maggie." Another pause. Jack glanced at her empty wine glass. "You want another?" Maggie considered. "No." Jack nodded. He seemed to debate something, then pulled his phone from his pocket. "Look," he said, shifting his weight. "I don't know what this is—" He gestured vaguely between them. "—or if it's anything at all. But I'd like to call you sometime." Maggie inhaled slowly. A door. Just barely cracked open. She could step through, or she could let it close again. For a moment, she wasn't sure what she wanted. But then—without thinking too hard—she reached into her clutch and pulled out one of the business cards she still had from her HR days. Jack took it without looking at it, just watching her. "Still carry these around?" he asked, his voice light but careful. "Only for special occasions," she said. Jack huffed a quiet laugh, slipping the card into his pocket. A beat passed. Then, before either of them could talk themselves out of it, Jack cleared his throat. "I fly out tomorrow morning." Maggie nodded, as if she already knew. Jack hesitated, then took a small step forward. "You feel like grabbing coffee before I go?" Maggie tilted her head slightly. She could say no. Could let this be the last moment between them, a polite nod to the past before they went their separate ways. But instead, she found herself saying, "Yeah. I think I do." Jack's mouth quirked into something that wasn't quite a smile, but wasn't not one either. "Alright then," he said. And for some reason, Maggie believed him.

CHAPTER SIX

He had no idea if she'd actually show up.

Hell, maybe she shouldn't. The café door swung open.

Jack glanced up.

And there she was.

Maggie stepped out, sunglasses perched on her nose, coffee cup in hand. Her hair was loose around her shoulders, and she was dressed casually—jeans and a soft blue sweater—but somehow, she still looked completely put-together.

Jack whistled quietly to himself, watching as she approached.

"Didn't think you'd come," he admitted.

Maggie smirked, taking a sip of coffee. "Neither did I."

She stopped a few feet away, tilting her head slightly. "You always this talkative in the morning?"

Jack chuckled, shaking his head. "Not unless I have to be."

A beat of silence.

The parking lot was quiet, save for the occasional passing car.

Maggie tapped her fingers against her cup. "So. Atlanta?"

Jack nodded. "Yeah." He glanced at his watch. "Couple hours."

Maggie exhaled, shifting her weight. "You like it there?"

Jack shrugged. "It's fine. Only there during the season. Off-season,

I'm in Tennessee."

Maggie lifted a brow. "Tennessee? Huh."

Jack smirked. "What?"

"I don't know. I just pictured you somewhere else. Maybe Florida. Near the ocean."

Jack took a sip of his coffee. "Turns out I like quiet."

Maggie considered that. "Didn't see you as the quiet type."

Jack smiled slightly. "Didn't used to be."

She hummed, nodding.

Jack shifted his stance. "What about you? Phoenix always the plan?"

Maggie shook her head. "Not really. Got a job offer here in the '90s. Took it, figured I'd move on eventually. But... I didn't."

Jack nodded. "Husband didn't mind?"

Maggie huffed a small laugh. "No husband."

Jack blinked, tilting his head slightly. "Ever?"

"Nope." She took a slow sip of coffee, then added, "Came close a couple times. Never stuck."

Jack studied her, his expression unreadable. "Huh."

Maggie tilted her head, smirking slightly. "You sound surprised."

Jack lifted a shoulder. "I guess I just figured..." He trailed off, then shook his head. "Nah. Never mind."

Maggie let out a quiet laugh. "What? You assumed someone would've locked me down by now?"

"Something like that."

She arched a brow. "Well, what about you? Marriage, divorce, scandalous affairs?"

"Just the divorce."

Maggie nodded. "Kids?"

Jack hesitated for a fraction of a second before answering.

"Emily's 35. Lives in New York. We talk every now and then." He shifted his weight. "Ryan's 38."

Maggie caught something in his voice. "And?"

Jack rolled his shoulders slightly. "He's in the Army."

That gave her pause. "Where?"

Jack let out a slow breath. "Iraq."

Maggie blinked, absorbing that.

"Damn," she murmured. "That must be..." She trailed off, because what was the right word for that?

Jack just nodded, glancing out toward Camelback Mountain, where the early light stretched across its ridges. "Yeah."

Jack took another sip of coffee. "You ever think about leaving? Going somewhere else?"

Maggie inhaled, shifting her weight.

"Sometimes," she admitted. "But then I ask myself... for what?"

Jack nodded, staring into his coffee.

They both knew what it felt like to stay in something because it was familiar.

Maggie finally sighed, lifting her chin. "And you? How many years you think you have left?"

Jack hesitated.

Not because he didn't know the answer.

But because he wasn't sure he wanted to say it out loud.

"I don't know how to do anything else," he admitted finally.

Maggie didn't react right away. Just studied him, turning the words over in her head.

She nodded once. "Yeah. I figured."

Jack glanced at her again. "I meant what I said the other night."

Maggie arched a brow. "You said a lot of things."

Jack smirked slightly. "I meant the part where I said I'd call."

Maggie studied him for a moment, then tilted her cup toward him in a small toast. "Then I guess I'll answer."

Jack let out a slow breath. "Yeah?"

Maggie smiled. "Yeah."

He wasn't sure what that meant.

But it was something.

And for now, that was enough.

CHAPTER SEVEN

1965 – Pittsburgh International Airport

Jack was twenty-six, in his prime, tearing up the outfield. He had a solid bat, quick enough hands in the outfield, and had spent the last three seasons as a solid starter with the Pirates.

He was waiting for a flight to Chicago when a group of college-aged guys spotted him across the terminal.

"Well, I'll be damned—Riggs!"

Jack looked up just as the tallest one nudged his friend, his face lighting up with recognition.

"We saw you play last weekend. That throw from the warning track? Hell of an arm."

Jack smirked, adjusting the brim of his cap. "Yeah? Thought I got lucky with that one."

"Lucky? Come on, you shoulda made the All-Star team," one of them said, shaking his head.

Jack let out a short chuckle. "Tell that to the voters."

They wanted autographs, so he signed. No problem.

1975 – Milwaukee Steakhouse

Jack, 36, two years retired, coaching some Podunk minor league team to because it just seemed like the thing you were to do.

He and some old teammates had gone out for dinner. The place was packed—nothing fancy, just a good steak joint with cold beer and big TVs.

At one point, the waiter—a kid who looked barely old enough to drink—brought their second round of beers and turned to Jack.

"You used to play, right?"

Jack set his glass down. "Yeah."

The kid nodded, but there was hesitation in his face.

"What was your name again?"

Jack's grip tightened slightly around the bottle.

He said it evenly, like it didn't bother him. "Jack Riggs."

The kid's eyes flickered with a hint of recognition, but it was fleeting.

"Oh, right—my dad used to talk about you. Said you were with the Brewers for a while."

Jack smirked, lifting his beer. "That's right. Your dad's got a good memory."

The kid grinned, then walked off to another table.

Jack didn't let it show, but something in him shifted.

2003 – Atlanta Braves Team Hotel, Phoenix

Now, at sixty-four, it was different.

He walked into the hotel bar late, still in his Braves polo from the game, rubbing a hand over the tension in his neck. The place was buzzing with the usual crowd—media guys, a few assistant coaches, and the younger women who always seemed to find their way to team hotels.

Jack took a seat at the bar and nodded at the bartender. "Bourbon, neat."

A few stools down, two women were sipping their drinks, watching the room the way people do when they're looking for someone.

Jack could feel their eyes move toward him.

One of them—a blonde in her late forties, maybe early fifties—tilted her head slightly. "You're with the team, right?"

Jack let out a slow breath. "Yeah."

The other one squinted. "You're… a coach?"

Jack nodded. "Third base."

That was where it ended now.

No mention of his playing days.

No holy cow, you were with the Pirates or I had your baseball card or I remember watching you play at County Stadium.

Just… a coach.

The blonde gave him a once-over, as her friend leaned in. "Not the manager, though," she murmured, like she was trying to figure out his level of importance.

Jack smirked into his bourbon.

He wasn't mad about it.

But it was something to sit with.

There had been a time—a long time ago—when walking into a place like this meant getting recognized, meant someone had a story about watching him play, meant an old fan would come up and say, "Man, you had a hell of a swing."

Now?

Now, he was just another guy in team gear sitting at the bar.

Jack could feel the blonde still assessing him, trying to decide if he was worth the effort.

Maybe ten years ago, she wouldn't have hesitated.

He wondered what she saw.

An older guy, sure, but still fit. Not washed up. Probably still had money, though not that kind of money—not the kind that made a woman lean in faster, offering her best laugh at something that wasn't all that funny.

Did she think he was lonely?

Maybe.

And maybe she wasn't wrong.

But hell, what did that say about him if he knew that and still played along?

Jack swirled the ice in his glass and lifted his gaze just enough to meet hers.

Her lips curved in something half-intrigued, half-expectant.

He could have smiled. Could have invited the moment to stretch out a little longer.

Instead, he knocked back the rest of his drink and turned away.

Jack swiped his key card and stepped into his hotel room, the door shutting behind him with a soft click.

The place was too neat, too quiet.

The air still held that artificial chill from the AC, the sheets tucked in too perfectly on the bed.

For a second, he just stood there.

Then, with a sigh, he pulled his phone out of his pocket, flipping it open with one hand.

He scrolled through his contacts, not really looking for anything, but not really stopping either.

Names he hadn't called in years.

Former teammates. Old coaches. A couple of guys from his playing days who had moved into broadcasting.

A few numbers of women he'd met in places just like this, all still saved even though he couldn't remember the last time he actually used them.

He paused when he got to Emily.

He hovered his thumb over her name for a second longer than he should have.

Then he kept scrolling.

Ryan.

Jack's jaw tightened.

Iraq.

There was nothing to say, nothing he could do, and even if there was, his son didn't want to hear it from him.

Jack exhaled slowly and moved past the name.

Then his thumb landed on Andrea.

His ex-wife.

He stared at the name for a long moment, his finger hovering over the call button.

He didn't want to talk to her. Hadn't wanted to talk to her for years.

But sometimes, she was still the first name that popped into his head when things felt off.

For years, even when the marriage was strained, they had been tethered together through the kids, through the schedule, through habit.

She used to call him out when he was full of shit. She never let him get away with much.

That was part of the reason it all fell apart in the end.

Jack let out a slow breath and snapped the phone shut.

He tossed it onto the nightstand and scrubbed a hand over his face.

Tomorrow, he'd fly back to Atlanta.

Baseball would keep him busy.

And for now, that would have to be enough.

CHAPTER EIGHT

Phoenix - 2003

Maggie stood in front of her bedroom mirror, hands on her hips, surveying the outfit she'd put together.

Simple black dress. A pair of low heels she hadn't worn in years. Pearl earrings, understated but classic.

Fine. It was fine.

She exhaled and smoothed a hand down the front of her dress.

It had been a long time since she put this much effort into getting ready.

She wasn't nervous—she wouldn't let herself be.

It was just a dinner.

With a perfectly respectable, well-adjusted man.

A retired pilot, for God's sake. A guy who had traveled the world, who still played golf regularly, who had been vouched for by Brenda.

"This is what people do," she muttered to herself, as if saying it out loud made it more true.

She wasn't even waiting for Jack to call. Not really.

But here she was, standing in front of a mirror, wondering if she still remembered how to do this.

Maggie turned to grab her purse, but her reflection caught her eye again.

For a moment, she saw herself as she used to be—when dates had been easy, when getting dressed up had felt fun.

Decades past.

She sighed, grabbed her purse, and walked out before she could talk herself out of it.

Tom arrived precisely on time.

Not early. Not late. Exactly when he said he would.

Maggie recognized that about him almost instantly—he was the kind of man who lived by schedule, by precision, by things happening when and how they were supposed to.

It made sense, given his career. Thirty years as a commercial pilot for TWA.

"Margaret," he greeted her, offering a firm but careful handshake.

"Maggie," she allowed, sliding into her seat.

Tom nodded, as if filing the information away for future reference.

He was polite, polished, with the kind of calm demeanor that probably reassured nervous passengers at 30,000 feet.

He didn't talk just to fill the silence. When he spoke, it was with purpose. Direct, succinct.

But unlike other men she had dated, he wasn't arrogant.

If anything, he was oddly formal.

Over drinks, Tom told her about his time flying transatlantic routes.

The long-haul flights to London, the early morning descents into LaGuardia, the precise timing it all required.

It was clear he loved the mechanics of it, the rhythm, the routine.

"It's the details," he said at one point, swirling his scotch. "Every flight, every route—it all comes down to the details. The smallest mistake at the wrong time, and everything changes."

Maggie nodded. "Sounds a little like my old job."

Tom tilted his head slightly. "HR?"

Maggie smiled. "You'd be surprised. One bad hire, one payroll error—suddenly, you've got a disaster on your hands."

Tom chuckled. "I suppose that's true."

But he didn't ask anything else.

Not about her career. Not about how she had ended up in Phoenix.

Not about what she did now that she was retired.

It wasn't that he dominated the conversation—he was too controlled for that.

But he talked about what he knew, what he understood.

And anything outside of that? He simply didn't think to ask.

Tom ordered another round of wine.

Maggie wasn't even finished with her first glass.

"So, what about you?" Tom said, leaning in slightly. "You said you used to work in HR. What made you pick that?"

Maggie blinked, caught slightly off guard.

Not because of the question, but because of how long it had taken him to ask.

She tilted her head, considering how to answer.

"I kind of fell into it," she admitted. "I took an entry-level role at a construction company in Memphis thinking I'd move into finance. But HR suited me. I liked the problem-solving. The structure of it. And people tend to underestimate HR—until they need it."

Tom nodded thoughtfully, but his gaze had already shifted—not away from her, exactly, but inward.

Like he was filing the information rather than engaging with it.

"Structure," he said finally. "That makes sense."

Maggie lifted a brow. "Does it?"

Tom gave her a small smile. "You strike me as someone who likes things to be ordered."

Maggie exhaled through her nose, amused despite herself. "You got that in one dinner?"

Tom chuckled. "Well, I did fly planes for thirty years. You need read co-workers quickly."

Maggie considered that.

He wasn't wrong.

But she couldn't shake the feeling that he was seeing the version of her that fit neatly into his view of the world—not the whole picture.

Tom walked her to her car.

Everything about him was steady, measured.

At one point, Maggie glanced at his wrist and wasn't surprised to see he still wore a pilot's watch.

A relic of a career he had left behind—but not really.

He was still operating by the same rules, the same precise timing.

Maybe that was why this wasn't working.

Not because he was a bad guy—he wasn't.

But because she could already see how it would go.

How he'd wake up at the same time every morning. How he'd expect predictability, order.

How he'd think that was a good thing.

And Maggie—Maggie wasn't sure she wanted predictable anymore.

"This was nice," Tom said, hands in his pockets, his tone just as even as it had been all night.

Maggie hesitated.

She could say it.

She could even mean it.

Instead, she just nodded. "Yeah. It was."

Tom hesitated for a beat, as if sensing something was off.

"Well," he said, still polite, still composed. "Maybe we can do it again sometime."

Maggie didn't commit to that either.

She just gave him a polite smile, thanked him for dinner, and got into her car.

The roads were quiet.

Maggie rolled down her window, letting the desert air rush in.

She should have enjoyed tonight.

She should have felt something.

But all she felt was a kind of tiredness she couldn't quite name.

Not boredom.

Not regret.

Just the sense that this was all too familiar.

She had been here before.

And it had never been enough.

And she drove home, feeling more alone than she had before the date even started.

CHAPTER NINE

The team had an off day before the start of the regular season, and Jack had nowhere to be.

It was the kind of afternoon he used to look forward to—the rare pause between games, where he could sleep in, grab a slow breakfast, go over some film with some players.

But now?

Now, he wasn't sure what to do with himself.

So, he found himself in the hotel lobby, nursing a cup of coffee, flipping through the paper, not really reading anything.

And, for whatever reason, his mind drifted back to Andrea.

His ex-wife.

The woman he had loved. Or maybe just the woman who had been willing to put up with him the longest.

Jack didn't hate her.

He didn't even blame her.

Not really.

Because, in the end, what did he expect?

1980 – The Beginning of the End

Jack had been forty-one, coaching for the Detroit Tiger's minor league team, thinking he had a future in the dugout.

Andrea had never been naïve about baseball life.

She knew what she signed up for.

She knew the travel, the long road trips, the late nights, the drinking, the women.

She knew about the women.

Maybe not all of them.

But enough.

And for a while, she didn't ask questions.

Didn't make a fuss.

Because Jack was making real money back then.

And because, despite it all, she loved him.

But when he started slowing down on the field—when it became clear that his career wasn't going to last much longer—the cracks widened.

Because money wasn't going to get any bigger.

Because the adoration that had kept him feeling important was starting to fade.

Because Jack—deep down—wasn't sure who he was without baseball.

And Andrea?

She saw it before he did.

Jack had tried.

For a while.

He had stopped messing around—at least, as far as Andrea knew.

He had tried to be home more in the off-season, tried to be the husband he was supposed to be.

But it wasn't enough.

Because the truth was, he had never been home, even when he was there.

Even in the same house, his mind had been on baseball.

On spring training. On the next season. On whether or not he could squeeze out one more contract before his legs finally gave out.

He had never pictured retirement.

Because he never thought it would happen to him.

Until, suddenly, it did.

And by then, Andrea had checked out.

The moment Jack stopped playing, she stopped pretending.

She wanted a divorce.

And Jack, deep down, knew she was right to ask for it.

The settlement had been brutal.

Not because Andrea bled him dry—she hadn't.

But because he hadn't saved like he should have.

He hadn't been reckless, but he had lived the way ballplayers did— big houses, nice cars, throwing money at things without thinking about the future.

Because when you're twenty-five and still playing, you think there's always more coming.

And then, suddenly, there isn't.

Jack had walked away with enough to thrive on, but not enough to coast forever.

And the worst part?

He had no clue what else to do.

Baseball was all he knew.

And so, he got into coaching.

Not because he had some great passion for teaching the game.

But because he didn't know where else to go.

Jack stared down at his coffee.

Divorced almost fifteen years now.

Still working. Still grinding out a baseball life that didn't have much left to offer him.

He hadn't seen Andrea in years.

Hadn't wanted to.

But sometimes, he wondered—if he had been different, if he had been better, if he had stopped chasing baseball long enough to be an actual husband—would it have mattered?

Jack sighed, shaking his head.

No.

He had never been built for anything steady.

And that was the damn truth.

Opening Day at Turner Field, Atlanta – March 2003

The sun was blazing down on the infield, the sky that kind of perfect, uninterrupted blue that only seemed to happen on days like this—Opening Day, the fresh start, the illusion that everything was still in front of them.

Jack stood on the foul line with the rest of the Braves' coaching staff, his hands clasped behind his back, his gaze fixed somewhere just past the outfield wall as the pregame ceremony unfolded around him.

This part never changed.

Every team, every uniformed personnel—coaches, trainers, clubhouse guys—lined up along the baseline, introduced one by one.

The roar of the crowd louder for some than others.

Jack had been through this countless times—as a player, as a coach. He knew the rhythm of it.

And still, there was something about this day—the first game of the season, the moment before the real grind started—that made it all feel just a little different.

Not nerves.

Not exactly.

But something else.

Something he didn't want to name.

"Now introducing your Atlanta Braves coaching staff!"

Jack's name was called.

A polite round of applause. Nothing special.

It was always that way for the third-base coach—unless you were a legend, or a longtime staple of the organization, no one really cared.

He glanced down the line toward Bobby Cox, the man who had been running the Braves for almost two decades now.

Cox got a real ovation. A name that meant something in baseball.

Jack?

He was just part of the machine.

One of the gears. Replaceable.

He shifted slightly as the last of the introductions wrapped up.

The crowd stood.

The first notes of the national anthem rang out over Turner Field.

Jack kept his eyes forward.

For the first time in years, he let himself wonder how many more times he'd get to do it.

Jack was 64 years old.

Not ancient by baseball standards—hell, Bobby was 61, and Frank Robinson was still managing at 66.

But Bobby was a legend.

Frank was a Hall of Famer.

And Jack?

Jack was just a guy who had never been notable enough for another job to be guaranteed.

He'd been coaching with the Braves for eleven years.

Not because he was some genius in the dugout.

Not because teams were lining up to hire him.

But because he'd been here long enough to be useful, reliable.

He was good at his job.

But not special.

And when the Braves eventually let him go—because that was always the way it went—who was going to hire a 64-year-old third-base coach without a name that carried weight?

Jack swallowed, shifting his stance.

The anthem was still playing, but his mind was somewhere else now.

The baseball world had changed.

The young guys were flooding in.

Former players barely out of their 30s, taking coaching roles because they had the name recognition, the front-office connections.

The next wave was coming.

And if Jack was honest, he wasn't sure he'd survive it.

The moment passed.

The anthem ended, the crowd erupted, and the players hustled back to the dugout, the air electric with Opening Day energy.

Jack fell into step with the other coaches, heading toward the dugout.

Someone clapped him on the shoulder—one of the younger coaches, early 40s, a former big-leaguer who'd gotten into coaching straight out of retirement.

"Ready for another one, Riggs?"

Jack forced a smirk. "Hell, I don't have a choice."

The guy laughed, jogging ahead to talk to the pitching coach.

Jack stepped into the dugout, resting one hand against the padded railing, watching as the first batter of the game strode to the plate.

Baseball was about longevity. Survival.

And Jack had survived longer than most.

But for the first time in his career, he felt it—the clock ticking.

CHAPTER ELEVEN

Maggie sat on her back patio, a half-finished cup of coffee growing cold on the table beside her.

The morning air was cool, crisp, the last breath of spring before Phoenix settled into its summer furnace.

Her phone sat face-up on the table, Tom's number still in her recent calls.

She hadn't gotten back to him yet.

Hadn't decided if she was going to.

It wasn't that the date had been bad.

Tom had been polite. Charming. Perfectly decent company.

But...

That was the problem.

He had been fine.

And Maggie was starting to think she wasn't interested in fine.

Her phone buzzed—Brenda.

Maggie sighed, picking it up. Better to get this over with now.

"Good morning," she answered, leaning back in her chair.

"Well?" Brenda demanded, skipping past the pleasantries.

Maggie played coy. "Well, what?"

Brenda groaned. "Mags, come on. Tom. Are you seeing him again?"

Maggie glanced at the coffee cup, tracing the rim with her fingertip.

"He was nice," she said.

A beat of silence.

Then Brenda made a low, knowing noise.

"Oh, no," she said dramatically. "I know that voice. That's the 'he was nice, but' voice."

Maggie huffed. "It's not—"

"It is," Brenda cut in. "Come on, I've known you too long. What's wrong with him?"

Maggie sighed.

"Nothing," she admitted. "That's the thing. There's nothing wrong with him. He's—"

Perfectly fine.

Nice. Polished. Predictable.

And I felt absolutely nothing.

Brenda sighed. "Mags."

Maggie pinched the bridge of her nose. "Look, I don't know. Maybe I'm just out of practice."

Brenda was quiet for a moment. Then—softer now—she said, "Or maybe you just don't want to settle."

Maggie's stomach twisted.

Settle.

God, had she spent so long being single that she'd forgotten what it felt like to want someone?

Or was she just waiting for something she couldn't name?

Brenda clicked her tongue. "You don't have to see him again, you know."

"I know," Maggie murmured.

"Just don't talk yourself into it because you think you should."

Maggie sighed, staring out at the mountain ridge in the distance. "I won't."

And this time, she meant it.

Later that afternoon, she found herself cleaning out a kitchen drawer, one of those odd projects she always put off until she couldn't anymore.

Junk drawer. Filled with old takeout menus, loose rubber bands, batteries she wasn't sure even worked anymore.

She was about to toss an expired coupon when she saw it— Tom's business card.

US Airways, Retired.

Maggie picked it up, running her thumb over the embossed letters.

It felt like a business transaction.

That was what had felt off about the date.

It had been two professionals, exchanging information, checking boxes.

Even when he had leaned in, when he had smiled—it had all been measured, careful.

She was pretty sure Tom would have had the exact same date with any woman who fit into his world.

And Maggie?

She wasn't sure she wanted to fit into anyone's pre-planned life.

She held the card between her fingers for a moment longer.

Then she tossed it into the trash.

And she felt lighter for it.

CHAPTER TWELVE

Spring 1958 – Nashville, Tennessee

The sound of metal cleats against pavement was something Maggie would always associate with Jack Riggs. Even before she'd really known him—before she'd sat next to him in their freshman economics class, before she'd found herself lingering outside the baseball stadium, watching him at practice—she could hear him coming. She was sitting on the grass just outside Vanderbilt's Hawkins Field, a notebook open in her lap, though she'd long since given up pretending to study. It was warm, the kind of April afternoon that smelled like damp earth and freshly cut grass, and she could hear the distant crack of bat meeting ball from inside the stadium.

She wasn't here for Jack, not exactly. She was a sophomore, business and psych, dreaming of something bigger than Nashville, until Jack Riggs walked in.

She'd told herself she liked studying outside, that the baseball field was just a good spot. And yet— "There you are." Maggie looked up just as Jack's shadow stretched across her notebook. He was still wearing his Vanderbilt jersey, gray baseball pants streaked with dirt, a wooden bat slung over his shoulder.

The sight of him like this—sweaty, sunburned, grinning like

he'd just won something—was something she would always remember. "Been looking for me?" she teased, tilting her head. Jack smirked, setting his bat down and flopping onto the grass beside her. "Nah," he said, tossing his glove onto his chest. "But it's nice to know you're always here." Maggie scoffed, nudging him with her knee. "I am not always here." "Sure," Jack drawled, stretching his arms behind his head. "And I just happen to see you outside the stadium every other day." Maggie rolled her eyes, but her cheeks warmed. Jack watched her for a second, then smirked again. "You ever gonna come to a game?" he asked, voice casual. Maggie hesitated. "Maybe," she said. Jack huffed. "Maybe?" Maggie smiled, turning back to her notebook, though she wasn't really reading anything. "If you ask me nicely, maybe I'll consider it." Jack laughed—a real, warm sound that made her stomach flip. "Oh, Maggie Callahan," he murmured. "You're trouble." Maggie had told herself it wasn't a date.

Jack had told her the same thing when he showed up outside her dorm, hands in his pockets, grinning like he already knew she'd say yes.

"Come on," he'd said, rocking back on his heels. "Let's go get something to eat."

She'd hesitated, just long enough to pretend she had to think about it, then grabbed her bag and followed him down the sidewalk.

They ended up at a tiny, hole-in-the-wall diner off campus, the kind of place that smelled like fryer grease and cheap coffee, where the waitresses didn't bother with menus because they expected you to just know.

Jack did.

Maggie didn't, so she let him order for her.

"Two cheeseburgers, fries, and a chocolate milkshake," Jack told the waitress, flashing that lazy grin of his.

Maggie arched a brow as the woman walked away. "A milkshake?"

Jack leaned forward, resting his forearms on the table. "Trust me."

Maggie sat back, folding her arms. "That's a lot of confidence in one sentence."

Jack smirked. "Yeah, well. I'm a confident guy."

She huffed, shaking her head, but she was smiling.

Jack was comfortable in his own skin in a way most guys their age weren't. It wasn't cocky, not exactly—just an easy kind of self-assurance.

Like he knew exactly who he was, what he wanted, and how to get it.

"So," Jack said after a beat, tilting his head. "Tell me something about yourself I don't already know."

Maggie narrowed her eyes. "That depends. What do you already know?"

Jack tapped his fingers against the table, pretending to think. "Well. I know you always sit outside Hawkins Field, even though you pretend it's just a coincidence."

Maggie rolled her eyes. "It is."

Jack ignored her. "I know you're good at school, but not obnoxious about it. You're from Louisville—"

She blinked, surprised. "How'd you remember that?"

Jack just smirked. "I listen."

Maggie pressed her lips together, trying not to let that fluster her.

"And," Jack continued, "I know that you pretend not to care about baseball, but you do. At least a little."

Maggie lifted a brow. "That so?"

Jack leaned back, smirking like he'd won something. "You wouldn't be here if you didn't."

Their food arrived, and Jack immediately pulled the milkshake toward them, pushing it into the center of the table.

Maggie hesitated.

Jack grinned. "Come on, Callahan. Just one sip."

She narrowed her eyes. "If this is disgusting, I swear to God—"

Jack held up a hand. "I'm hurt that you don't trust me."

Maggie rolled her eyes, grabbed the straw, and took a sip.

It was delicious.

Jack watched her reaction, then grinned.

"I hate that you're right," she muttered, setting the shake down.
Jack laughed, shaking his head.
And that was how it started.

CHAPTER THIRTEEN

Maggie never thought she'd fall in love with a baseball player. She wasn't the type of girl who wasted time fawning over athletes. She had plans—a career to build, a life to shape. And then Jack Riggs happened.

Or, rather—Jack Riggs didn't give her a choice.

Because Jack was the kind of guy who burrowed under your skin before you even knew he was there.

And by the time she figured it out, it was too late.

It was mid-June, and the air had turned cool and crisp, the kind of autumn weather that made you want to walk a little slower, breathe a little deeper.

Maggie and Jack were stretched out on a blanket in Centennial Park, half-watching the stars, half-listening to the distant hum of a street musician playing something soft on an acoustic guitar.

Jack had gone 4/4 that day, and he was still a little loose-limbed, the way he always was after a good game.

Maggie had been at that game.

She didn't go to all of them, but she went to enough.

At first, she told herself she was just supporting her friends—a few of the girls in her dorm had started going, and it was a fun way to spend an afternoon.

But she knew better now.

Jack had been watching for her in the stands.

And she had been watching him back.

Now, he lay on his back, arms folded behind his head, one leg bent at the knee.

Maggie was curled up beside him, her fingers trailing absentmindedly along the inside seam of his sweatshirt.

They were comfortable like this.

Which was maybe the strangest part—how easy it all was.

Jack didn't make her feel like she had to prove herself.

She didn't have to be the smartest person in the room, the most put-together, the most ambitious.

She could just be.

"You're thinking too hard," Jack murmured.

Maggie smiled, tilting her head toward him. "I'm always thinking too hard."

Jack hummed. "That's true."

She nudged him with her knee, and he chuckled, tilting his head to look at her.

He was quiet for a long moment.

Then, suddenly—soft, sure, like he wasn't even thinking about it—he said it.

"I love you."

Maggie froze.

For a second, she wasn't sure she'd heard him right.

Jack just kept looking at her, completely unbothered by the weight of what he'd just said.

Like he'd known for a while now.

Like he hadn't even considered not telling her.

Maggie opened her mouth, then closed it.

And for the first time in her life—she wasn't sure what to say.

Jack's mouth quirked up at the corner.

"That's a hell of a reaction," he teased.

Maggie huffed out a laugh, shaking her head. "No, I—" She swallowed, searching for the right words.

Jack just waited.

Because that was the thing about him.

He never pushed, never rushed her.

He just let her come to him.

And so she did.

Maggie exhaled, letting herself sink into the moment.

She reached out, tracing a fingertip along the sharp edge of his jaw.

And then—finally, fully, honestly—she said it back.

"I love you too."

Jack grinned—that easy, wide, Jack Riggs grin.

And then he kissed her—slow and steady, like he already knew they'd have forever.

CHAPTER FOURTEEN

Spring 1960 – Nashville, Tennessee

She was waiting for him outside his apartment, leaning against the hood of her car, arms folded across her chest.

Jack was late.

Again.

It wasn't like him—not before. Jack was always on time.

But lately, things had shifted.

First, it was the meetings, the workouts, the scouts pulling him into conversations that left him grinning like he had the whole world in front of him.

Then, it was the phone calls he didn't return right away.

And now?

Now he was late to their dates.

Maggie exhaled sharply, shaking her head as she checked her watch again.

She was about to leave when the door swung open, and Jack came jogging out—hair damp, shirt wrinkled like he'd just thrown it on, that same easy grin plastered across his face.

"Hey, hey, I'm here," he said, already trying to charm his way out of it.

Maggie narrowed her eyes. "You're late."

Jack grimaced, rubbing the back of his neck. "I know. I got caught up—"

"With baseball," Maggie finished flatly.

Jack paused.

Then sighed, stepping closer. "Yeah."

Maggie searched his face, looking for something, anything, that told her she wasn't about to get left behind.

But Jack just tilted his head, smiling like she was making too big a deal out of it.

"Come on," he said, sliding an arm around her waist. "Let's go. We'll have a good night, yeah?"

Maggie wanted to be mad.

But when Jack was like this—warm, close, his lips brushing the side of her head like he could feel her hesitation—how was she supposed to fight it?

She sighed, letting herself lean into him.

But as they got into the car, she couldn't help but wonder—

How much longer was she going to let him pull her back in?

CHAPTER FIFTEEN

Maggie had always known Jack Riggs would play professional baseball.

It wasn't just his talent—though he had plenty of that. It was the way he carried himself, the way he talked about the game, the way he never entertained the idea of a future without it.

So when his name was called in the fourth round of the draft, when he became a professional ballplayer in an instant, she shouldn't have been surprised.

And yet—she still felt breathless.

Because this wasn't just his dream.

It was theirs.

Or at least, it had been.

Jack was pacing his apartment, barefoot, holding a beer he kept forgetting to drink.

The draft had started hours ago, and they had been waiting.

Waiting for the phone to ring.

Waiting for his name to be called.

Waiting to find out where their future was going to start.

Maggie had never seen Jack like this—nervous, restless.

Jack Riggs was always confident. Always so sure.

But tonight, his fingers tapped against the neck of the bottle, his jaw tightened every time another name was announced.

Maggie sat cross-legged on his couch, watching him.

"You should eat something," she said.

Jack snorted. "I should get drafted."

She smiled, but before she could tease him back—

The phone rang.

Jack froze.

For the first time all night, he was completely still.

Then, with a sharp inhale, he set the beer down without looking, nearly knocking it over, and grabbed the receiver.

"Yeah?"

A pause.

Then—his whole face changed.

Maggie didn't have to hear the other side of the conversation.

She knew.

Jack lit up, his grin slow and wide, the kind of smile that made you want to stand close just to feel the warmth of it.

"Yeah," he said, voice breathless. "Yeah, I'm here."

Maggie sat completely still.

Because this was it.

The moment that changed everything.

She should have been thrilled.

And in a way—she was.

But somewhere, in the back of her mind, a small voice whispered something she wasn't ready to hear.

This is where you lose him.

Jack Riggs was no longer just Jack.

He was a professional baseball player.

CHAPTER SIXTEEN

Summer 1961

Maggie hadn't seen Jack in awhile.

Not since the calls slowed to a trickle and then stopped altogether. Not since she stopped driving to see him in whatever city he'd been assigned to that season. Not since she realized that Jack Riggs wasn't waiting for her anymore.

Four years was a long time when you were in your twenties.

Long enough to build a new life.

Long enough to almost forget the feeling of waiting on someone who had already left.

But then, the Nashville Vols hosted Jack's farm team.

And there he was.

And Maggie had to see it for herself.

She told herself it was curiosity.

Nothing more.

But as she sat in the stands of Suplhur Dell, watching Jack take his spot in the outfield, she knew that was a lie.

She wasn't just curious.

She was testing something.

She wanted to see if it still hurt.

And as she watched him—the way he moved, the way he still carried himself—she realized something.

It didn't.

Not the way it used to.

There was still an ache, sure.

But it wasn't sharp anymore.

It wasn't a wound. Just a scar.

Jack Riggs had once been the most important thing in her world.

And now?
Now he was just a man playing baseball.
And Maggie?
She wasn't waiting anymore.
Not for him.
Not for anyone.

She could have waited for him after the game.
Could have stood near the player's exit, waited for that moment when his eyes landed on her.
Could have forced a reunion, a conversation, a chance for him to prove her wrong.
But she already knew how it would go.
Jack would see her, and for a moment, he'd smile.
For a moment, it would be like old times.
And then he'd remember who he was now.
And she'd remember who she had become without him.
She didn't need to hear him say it.
She didn't need him to tell her that baseball still came first.
She already knew.
So, she stood.
Brushed peanut shells off her jeans.
And walked out of the stadium before the game was even over.
And it was the easiest thing she had ever done.

CHAPTER SEVENTEEN

Spring 2003

Maggie wasn't actually looking to move.

She liked her house well enough—a quiet little place in a neighborhood where no one bothered her but would wave if they saw her walking the dog. It was comfortable, settled, familiar.

But ever since she retired, she'd started doing this thing.

Going to open houses on Sundays.

Just for fun.

It had started on accident—a random detour after brunch with Brenda, a passing curiosity about how the other half lived.

Then it became a habit.

She told herself it wasn't serious.

She wasn't one of those people who needed a big change to feel like she was moving forward.

But still, every Sunday, she found herself wandering through some newly listed property, sipping complimentary lemonade, nodding politely as a realtor talked about square footage and vaulted ceilings.

And today was no different.

The house was nice. Bigger than hers. More modern. More expensive. It had big windows, the kind that let the Arizona sun flood in, making everything feel open and bright. The kitchen was beautiful—all stainless steel and granite, the kind of kitchen people said they wanted and then never actually cooked in. Maggie wandered through it, trailing her fingers along the counter.

"You thinking of buying?"

She turned to see a realtor smiling at her.

Maggie smiled back. Shook her head.

"Just looking."

The woman gave her a knowing nod. "I get that a lot."

Maggie wasn't sure what made her say it, but before she could stop herself, she said, "I used to do this with my mom when I was younger."

The realtor tilted her head. "Oh yeah?"

Maggie nodded, letting herself remember.

"She liked to look at houses she'd never actually buy. We'd go to these big, fancy open houses, walk through like we belonged there, and imagine what life would be like."

It had been a game.

Her mom would pick a room—say, the kitchen or the backyard or the massive walk-in closet—and make up a story about the people who lived there.

That had been the fun part. Imagining the life that went with the house.

And now?

Now Maggie was walking through these houses alone.

Still imagining.

But instead of picturing a perfect little family, a couple picking out paint colors together, kids running through the halls—

She was trying to imagine herself.

And she wasn't sure if she liked what she saw.

Maggie wandered into the living room, pretending she wasn't

thinking too hard.

And that's when she saw him.

David Carter.

Her old boss's right-hand man.

Retired, like she was.

And apparently, also spending his time at open houses.

"Maggie Callahan?" His eyebrows lifted as he approached. "Well, I'll be damned."

Maggie laughed, shaking his hand. "David, what are you doing here?"

"What, a man can't look at million-dollar houses he has no intention of buying?"

She grinned. "So we have the same hobby."

David chuckled. "Guess so. But seriously—you thinking about a move?"

Maggie hesitated.

Because was she?

"I don't know," she admitted. "I don't think so. Just... passing time."

David nodded. "Yeah. Retirement'll do that to you."

He slipped his hands into his pockets, looking around the room. "You ever think about doing something meaningful with your time? Even part-time?" Maggie blinked. "Meaningful?"

David smirked. "I mean actual work. Consulting. Using that brain of yours."

Maggie snorted. "Now you sound like my old boss."

David shrugged, a knowing look in his eye. "Well, I've got something that might interest you. I'm on the board of a non-profit—Phoenix Futures Initiative. They do workforce development, helping people get back on their feet. Training, job placement, career guidance. The whole deal."

Maggie hesitated. That actually sounded... interesting.

David pulled a business card from his pocket, holding it out to her. "We could use someone like you, even just as an advisor. Think about it."

Maggie took the card, her fingers tracing over the embossed logo.

Phoenix Futures Initiative.

For some reason, the name nagged at something in the back of her mind.

She just didn't know why.

Yet.

CHAPTER EIGHTEEN

Spring 2003, Somewhere along Interstate 40

The plan was loose.

Drive east, maybe go all the way to Santa Fe if they felt like it. Stop at whatever caught their eye along the way.

Brenda had mapped out a few places—a winery, an artsy little town, some hot springs she swore were worth the drive.

Maggie just went along with it.

They drove with the windows down, music from a classic rock station humming through the car.

It was easy, relaxed.

Brenda talked about her husband, about her grandkids, about how her daughter was driving her crazy.

And Maggie?

Maggie just listened.

Until Brenda finally turned the conversation toward her.

"So," Brenda said, adjusting her sunglasses. "Are we gonna talk about it?"

Maggie blinked. "Talk about what?"

Brenda shot her a look. "Don't play dumb, Mags. You've been off ever since the game."

Maggie sighed, shifting in her seat. "I'm fine."

Brenda snorted. "Yeah, yeah, sure. Totally fine. That's why you've been brooding like a woman in a country song for the last two weeks."

Maggie rolled her eyes, but Brenda wasn't letting it go.

"It's about Jack, isn't it?"

Maggie kept her gaze firmly on the road.

"It's not about Jack," she lied.

Brenda huffed out a laugh.

"Maggie. I've known you for how many years? You're not exactly subtle."

Maggie tightened her grip on the wheel.

Because what was she supposed to say?

That she had spent the last three decades assuming Jack Riggs was just a piece of her past—some story from her twenties she barely thought about anymore?

And then she saw him standing there in the third-base coach's box and suddenly she was twenty-three again, waiting for him to look at her.

It was stupid.

It was so, so stupid.

Brenda let the silence stretch for a few beats before speaking again.

"Did you love him?"

Maggie glanced at her.

Brenda wasn't teasing now.

She was serious.

And Maggie didn't have an answer.

Not one that made sense.

So instead, she just said—

"I don't know."

Brenda didn't press.

She just nodded, like she understood something Maggie didn't.

And they kept driving.

Phoenix

The first time Jack reached out, Maggie wasn't expecting it.

It was the Monday after the charity event, and she was standing in the checkout line at Safeway, flipping through a magazine she had no intention of buying, when her phone buzzed in her bag.

She dug it out, only half paying attention, expecting it to be Brenda or maybe a robocall trying to sell her a car warranty.

Instead—Jack Riggs.

The last time she'd seen that name pop up on her phone, it had been sitting on a business card she didn't think he'd actually use.

She let it ring twice before answering.

"Didn't think I'd hear from you," she said, grabbing her grocery bags and moving toward the exit.

"Didn't think I'd call," Jack admitted.

Neither of them said anything right away.

Jack was the one to break the pause. "Figured I should check in. Seeing as how we're old friends and all."

Maggie snorted. "That what we are?"

Jack let out a quiet chuckle, and there was something about it— something real—that made Maggie hesitate.

"I don't know," he said finally. "But I do know that when I saw you the other night, I didn't hate it."

Maggie swallowed, pushing open the glass door, stepping into the late-March warmth of the Phoenix evening.

"Guess I can't argue with that," she murmured.

She was about to say something else, but Jack beat her to it.

"All right, Mags. Just wanted to say hey."

Mags.

She closed her eyes briefly.

"Hey back," she said.

And then he hung up.

No goodbye. No plan to talk again.

But somehow, Maggie knew that wouldn't be the last time.

After that, there wasn't a pattern, exactly.

Jack would email every so often. Not daily. Not even every week. Just when he felt like it.

And Maggie would answer.

Never right away. Never with more than a few words at a time.

But she answered.

JACK: Saw a guy at the ballpark in an old Vanderbilt cap. Thought of you.

MAGGIE: He must be a very patient man.

JACK: Or just bad at letting things go.

Maybe she'd start following baseball again.

Not because of Jack.

Of course not.

But because she had too much time on her hands, and people in Phoenix seemed to care about the Diamondbacks. It wouldn't be the worst thing to have a team to root for, something to pay attention to while she figured out how to fill her days.

She told herself that was all it was as she sat at her kitchen table, sipping her morning coffee, flipping through the sports section.

The Diamondbacks' opening series was against the Dodgers. Good. That was something. A rivalry. A reason to tune in.

She folded the paper, set it aside.

Then hesitated.

She unfolded it again.

Not because of Jack.

Just... because she'd seen something on TV the other night about how the Braves were expected to do this season.

And maybe she was curious.

She flipped a few pages, scanning quickly, just to see.

Braves Opening Day – March 31st – Atlanta vs. Montreal.

She barely lingered on the line before shutting the paper completely.

She wasn't looking it up because of Jack.

She just liked to know things.

That was all.

And maybe she'd watch the Diamondbacks game that week.

Maybe.

The Diamondbacks game wasn't on yet.

That's what she told herself when she picked up the remote.

She'd meant to watch them. Get

invested, learn a few player names, maybe even have something to talk about with people who still cared about that kind of thing.

It was a distraction. A hobby.

And if she had to sit through a few national games on ESPN before the Diamondbacks broadcast started, then so be it.

She wasn't choosing this.

She was just killing time.

That's all.

And when the Braves games began, she didn't change the channel.

Maggie hadn't watched a baseball broadcast in years.

She didn't know who any of the players were, didn't recognize the broadcasters' voices. She barely remembered how long games took, or what the rules were.

She wasn't really paying attention, just half-listening as the broadcast rolled through pregame ceremonies, the kind of grand, patriotic spectacle that baseball loved to put on. She leaned back against the couch, fingers resting lightly on the remote.

Then the camera panned across them, and there he was—older, sharper, standing still in a row of younger men in crisp white uniforms.

Jack Riggs.

Her stomach tightened.

She barely noticed the details of the shot—the way the flag rippled behind them, the faces of the other coaches and players standing beside him.

She just saw him.

The way he stood there, composed, serious. The way the camera lingered on him just long enough for her to take it all in.

Then the broadcast moved on before she was ready.

Maggie let out her breath, reached for her glass of water, tried to act like she hadn't been waiting for it.

She left the game on, let it play in the background while she folded laundry.

But when the cameras cut to a shot of the Braves dugout, and she saw him again—leaning against the railing, studying the field, lost in his own world—

She turned the TV off.

And sat there.

Because suddenly, she didn't feel like watching baseball anymore.

CHAPTER NINETEEN

Maggie adjusted her sunglasses and stepped out of her car, glancing up at the modest but modern-looking office building in downtown Phoenix.

Phoenix Futures Initiative.

The place looked the part.

A clean glass entryway, neatly printed brochures in the lobby, a receptionist who smiled a little too brightly.

If Maggie hadn't worked in corporate hiring for decades, she might have been impressed.

Instead, she took it all in with quiet skepticism.

She still wasn't sure why she was here.

She had emailed David Carter a week ago, expecting a casual coffee meeting. Instead, he had fast-tracked her straight into a sit-down with the executive director.

It felt... a little eager.

But Maggie wasn't one to back down from something just because it moved quickly.

And besides, what else did she have to do?

The executive director was a woman named Laura Middleton, early 50s, with the look of someone who'd once been polished but was now barely holding things together. Her blazer was buttoned wrong, her desk a disaster of half-sorted files and coffee cups, and when she stood to greet Maggie, she knocked over a pen and immediately lost track of it.

She had the frantic energy of someone trying to stay three steps ahead but constantly tripping over her own feet.

"Maggie! Great to meet you," she said too brightly, shaking her hand a little too hard. "I've heard fantastic things."

That was the first thing that struck Maggie as odd.

She hadn't done anything yet.

What exactly had David Carter told them?

Laura gestured toward the chair across from her desk. "Sit, sit, please. Uh, ignore the mess, I'm, uh—*reorganizing* things."

Maggie glanced around. Stacks of folders and half-empty coffee cups lined the desk. A PFI annual report sat on top of a *very* full trash bin.

Laura clasped her hands together, then immediately uncrossed them, shifting in her chair.

"So!" she said brightly. "I know you're, uh, just considering involvement, but we'd *love* to have someone like you on board. Your experience is exactly what we need."

Maggie kept her expression neutral. "How long has PFI been around?"

Laura blinked fast, like she hadn't expected the question.

"Oh! Uh—five years. Well, no, *technically* six, but, y'know, the first year was, like, small potatoes. Like, really tiny—like, 'operating out of a Starbucks' tiny—so, um, five that really *count,* I guess?" She let out a nervous laugh, waving a hand like she was erasing her own rambling. "But yeah. Five."

Maggie tucked that detail away.

Rapid expansion. Big money coming in fast.

Not always a red flag.

But not always a good sign, either.

Laura kept talking—too much, too fast.

"Oh, and our donors have been *phenomenal.* You would not *believe* the support we've gotten from—" she rattled off a few corporate sponsors, voice getting lighter, more animated as she spoke.

She was giving a pitch.

Maggie didn't interrupt.

She just listened.

Laura talked a lot about funding. Growth. Big plans.

Not much about actual results.

And that?

That was more interesting than anything she'd said so far.

By the end of the meeting, Maggie had agreed to a small consulting role. Just a few hours a week, reviewing hiring practices and employee retention.
Easy enough.
Before she left, Laura handed her a packet of documents to review.
And that was the second thing that struck Maggie as odd.
There was a lot of paperwork.
And almost all of it was about donor reports and financials.
Very little about actual job placements.
Still, she took the folder with a smile, shook Laura's hand, and walked out into the Phoenix heat.
As she slid into her car, she set the packet on the passenger seat and stared at it for a long moment.
It was probably nothing.
But something about the whole thing felt too polished.
Like a place that had memorized its own story.
She started the car and pulled onto the road.
Maybe she was just out of practice.
Maybe she'd spent too many years looking for what was wrong instead of trusting what was right.
Or maybe;
Maybe something here didn't quite add up.

CHAPTER TWENTY

June 2003, Phoenix

Maggie climbed down from the stepstool, stretching her arms as she looked over the fresh coat of paint.

"Not bad," Brenda said, stepping back to inspect it. "Are you sure you didn't miss your calling as a contractor?"

Maggie huffed a laugh. "Give me a few more houses to practice on, and we'll see."

Across the room, Mark was helping their son, Jason, tape off the baseboards. Jason, a sophomore in college, had inherited his dad's love of sports—which meant the two of them had spent the last twenty minutes swapping opinions on teams, stats, and which players were underperforming.

"You catching Sunday Night Baseball tomorrow?" Jason asked, pressing tape along the floorboards.

Mike nodded. "Yeah, Braves are playing, but it might be a clunker. They've been slumping bad."

Jason made a face. "How bad?"

Mike sighed. "Bad enough that ESPN's probably regretting putting them in prime time."

Maggie kept her expression neutral as she dipped the paintbrush back into the tray.

She wasn't following baseball.

Not really.

But she still heard that.

Brenda must have noticed the slight pause in her movements, because she nudged her with an elbow.

"You okay over there?"

Maggie forced a small chuckle. "Yeah. Just remembering why I never went into home improvement."

Brenda smirked. "Well, let's hope you don't ruin that corner, or else you'll be stuck doing another coat."

Maggie turned back to the wall, but the conversation behind her lingered.

Brenda crouched down, taping off the baseboards while Maggie started on another section of trim.

"So, are you actually gonna go back to work?" Brenda asked, glancing up.

Maggie shrugged. "Not full-time. But I took a meeting with a non-profit last week—Phoenix Futures Initiative."

Mike glanced over from where he was handing Jason another roll of tape. "David Carter's group?"

Maggie nodded. "Yeah. You know them?"

Mike shrugged. "Enough to know they've got a lot of money moving through."

Maggie gave him a sharp look. "Legitimate money?"

Mike smirked. "Wouldn't know. But they know how to attract donors. Big corporate connections."

Brenda leaned on her arm. "And they want you for what, exactly?"

Maggie grabbed a clean rag, wiping some stray paint from her wrist. "Consulting on hiring practices, workforce development strategies. Apparently, they're trying to expand, and they don't have anyone with real HR experience at the executive level."

Brenda whistled. "And they just handed you the keys to the castle?"

Maggie smirked. "Not quite. But they were eager. More eager than I expected."

Mike made a thoughtful noise. "Fast-growing nonprofits can be like that. They scale quickly, then realize they need structure."

Maggie nodded. "Exactly. If they're pulling in serious funding, they can't just hire people off vibes. They need real systems in place."

Brenda gave her a sideways look. "And you're not suspicious that they've made it this far without one?"

Maggie tapped her fingers against the paint can, considering. "I wouldn't say suspicious. But I know how these things go. The mission looks good, the donations are rolling in, but behind the scenes, people are flying blind."

Mike took a sip of his beer. "So what's your gut say? Legit operation, or PR house of cards?"

"Too soon to tell. But I'll know soon enough."

Brenda smirked. "You sound like you already made up your mind."

Maggie didn't respond. She hadn't. But she was getting there.

CHAPTER
TWENTY ONE

Early July 2003, New York City

Jack hated rainouts.

They threw off routines. They messed with travel schedules. They left too much damn time to think.

But today, he couldn't be mad about it.

The rain had started that morning, slow and steady, but by noon, Shea Stadium was a swamp. The game had been postponed hours before first pitch, and the team had scattered—some guys staying in, some heading into the city, some already drinking.

Jack did something else.

He called Emily.

And to his mild surprise, she picked up on the second ring.

"You calling 'cause you're bored or 'cause you actually wanted to see me?" she asked, amusement in her voice.

Jack smirked. "Can't it be both?"

Emily sighed, but he could hear the smile. "I'm free. Where are you?"

The rain was steady but not aggressive, blurring the edges of the city as Jack stepped onto the curb outside the team hotel.

Emily's car—a small, sensible sedan that didn't fit her at all—was pulled up to the front, hazard lights flashing.

Jack climbed in, brushing raindrops off his sleeves. "Didn't think I'd get the chauffeur treatment."

Emily scoffed. "Don't get used to it. This thing barely gets out of the garage."

Jack smirked. "That right?"

She nodded, flicking on her turn signal. "Yeah. I think I drive, like, five times a year. Only when I absolutely have to."

Jack chuckled, glancing around the interior. "So what, this is your annual warm-up lap?"

Emily shot him a dry look. "I live in New York, Dad. Ever heard of the subway?"

Jack huffed a small laugh. "Yeah, and you know what it smells like?"

Emily shook her head, merging into traffic. "So what's the deal? You're in town and suddenly feel like playing dad?"

Jack glanced out at the rain-slick streets.

"Just figured I'd take advantage of the rainout."

Emily arched a brow. "Mm-hmm."

Jack smirked. "What?"

Emily shook her head, not looking away from the road. "Nothing. Just not used to you having time to kill."

They ended up at a small café in Brooklyn, the kind of place Emily liked—small tables, indie music playing low, baristas who could talk about beans and microclimates the same way Jack could talk about baserunning.

Jack, still damp from the rain, stuck to black coffee. Emily ordered something iced, something with oat milk, something that sounded more like a dessert than a drink.

Jack watched her stir sugar into her cup, the way she was fully settled in her life here.

She had her own place, her own job, her own city.

And he didn't know any of it.

"How's work?" he asked.

Emily looked at him over the rim of her glass. "Good. Busy."

Jack waited for more, but that was all she offered.

She wasn't mad at him. Not exactly.

She just… didn't need him.

Emily tilted her head. "Okay, what's going on?"

Jack frowned. "What do you mean?"

"I mean, you called me. Voluntarily." She leaned forward slightly.

"Something's up."

"It's just... been a long season."

Emily studied him. "Bad year?"

Jack hesitated, then gave a small nod. "Something like that."

Emily didn't press.

But she knew.

She always knew.

She glanced toward the window, then back at him. "You ever think about what's next?"

Jack's throat tightened slightly.

No.

That was the problem.

He never had.

Jack forced a small smirk. "I was kind of hoping you'd let me crash on your couch."

Emily rolled her eyes but smiled. "Yeah, I'll pass on that."

Jack chuckled, but the weight in his chest didn't lift.

Because the truth was—he didn't have an answer to her question.

And he was starting to think he should.

Emily stirred the ice in her drink, watching him. "Have you talked to Mom lately?"

Jack huffed a quiet laugh. "Not unless you count lawyers."

Emily gave a knowing smirk. "Still?"

Jack rubbed a hand over his jaw. "She's thorough."

That got a snort. "That's one word for it."

They sat in silence for a moment, the rain drumming softly against the café window.

Emily looked down at her cup, her fingers tapping absently against the glass. "You know, for a long time, I thought she hated you."

Jack glanced at her, surprised. "Your mom?"

Emily nodded. "Yeah. When I was a kid, I figured silence meant hate, you know? After the divorce, she never talked about you unless she had to. No bitterness, no anger—just... nothing. And I hated it, Dad. I wanted her to care, because then maybe you'd care, too."

Jack exhaled, leaning back in his chair. "That sounds about right."

Emily tilted her head. "I think that was worse."

Jack frowned. "What do you mean?"

She hesitated, then shrugged. "I think if she'd yelled, or ranted about what a terrible husband you were, it would've meant she still cared. But she just shut it down. Like she turned off a switch and moved on."

Jack let out a slow breath, staring at the table. He knew Andrea had been done with him long before the divorce papers were signed.

It hadn't been dramatic. No screaming fights, no drawn-out scenes.

Just distance.

A slow, widening gap between them that he never really tried to close.

And maybe that was the problem.

Maybe she stopped trying, too.

Jack shifted, glancing up. "She ever say anything to you about it?"

Emily took a sip of her drink, considering. "Not much. Just that it was inevitable."

Jack swallowed. "Guess she wasn't wrong."

Emily met his gaze, her expression unreadable. "No. She wasn't."

Jack felt that one.

More than he wanted to admit.

For a moment, neither of them spoke.

Then, Emily leaned forward, elbows on the table. "Can I ask you something?"

Jack forced a smirk. "You've never needed permission before."

Emily rolled her eyes but didn't take the bait. "Did you ever love her?"

Jack blinked and coughed at the bluntness of the question.

That question landed harder than expected.

He could have said yes, obviously. He could have said of course.

But the truth was...

He didn't know how to answer.

Because it had never been simple.

Because love and effort weren't the same thing, and he had always been better at the first one than the second.

Jack exhaled, running a hand over his face. "I did. I just... didn't do a great job showing it."

Emily nodded, as if she had expected that answer.

She looked away, watching the rain outside.

Jack studied her for a moment, then sighed. "You ever talk to her?"

Emily shrugged. "Sometimes. Not often."

Jack hesitated. "She ever say anything about me?"

Emily turned back to him. "Not in years."

Jack nodded slowly.

Not surprising. But still, it sat heavy in his chest.

CHAPTER TWENTY TWO

The email came a few days into the renovation mess, just as Maggie was regretting every decision she'd made.

Subject: Still Surviving?
Maggie,
Still surviving Phoenix in July? Or have you finally melted?
Jack.

Subject: Re: Still Surviving?
Jack,
Barely. I'm convinced the heat is trying to kill me, but so far, I'm winning.
What about you? Still surviving a season that doesn't sound like much fun?
Maggie.

Subject: Re: Re: Still Surviving?
Maggie,
Winning is relative. The heat's not much different here in Atlanta, but at least I don't have to hear about it from half my roster every day.
As for the season... let's just say I've had better ones.
Jack.

Just enough.
Just little things.
The kind of easy, no-pressure back-and-forth that felt like slipping

into an old conversation without realizing you'd never really finished it.

The bedroom floors were next.
Which meant Maggie had to clear out the closet.
She was halfway through sorting old shoes and winter coats she never wore when she pulled out a dusty cardboard box, taped shut and shoved deep in the back.
She didn't recognize it at first.
Then she saw the handwriting scrawled on the side.
Vanderbilt
Maggie's breath caught.
She hesitated.
Then she sat down on the floor, pulled the tape off, and opened it.
Inside, she found a stack of old notebooks, a few college sweatshirts, ticket stubs, faded letters.
And beneath all of that—
A yellowed newspaper clipping from the Tennessean.
"Commodores Outfielder Jack Riggs Drafted by Pittsburgh in Fourth Round"
Her fingers hovered over the headline.
She hadn't seen this in decades.
She had forgotten she still had it.
Her eyes flicked over the photo—Jack at twenty-two, grinning under a Vanderbilt cap, standing with his bat slung over one shoulder.
For a moment, she could hear it all again.
The way he'd laughed when he told her the news.
The way he'd grabbed her hands and said, "Can you believe it?" like the world had just opened up.
The way she had believed, back then, that this meant they had a future.
Maggie let out a slow breath.
Then she folded the paper, tucked it back into the box, and pushed it aside.
Some things belonged in the past.

Even if the past had a way of sneaking back in.

CHAPTER TWENTY THREE

The All-Star Break (July 2003, Nashville, TN)

The MLB All-Star break was one of the only real pauses in the season. Three days without games, travel, or scouting reports—unless you were one of the guys who actually had to go.

Jack never had to go.

Twelve years in the big leagues, and not once was he named an All-Star.

One year—1970, maybe?—he'd been listed as an alternate. He got a call telling him to be ready in case someone backed out.

Nobody did.

That was baseball.

And that was Jack's career.

Good, but not great.

Not quite enough.

Jack let out a slow breath, dragging a hand down his face.

Maybe that was why Maggie had lingered in his mind so much lately.

She'd never cared about his stats or his contracts.

She'd known him before any of it.

Before baseball became the only thing that mattered.

She'd known the version of him that wasn't tied to a lineup card.

He wondered if she still saw that version.

Or if there was nothing left to see.

The flight home was short, barely long enough for him to close his eyes.

Nashville in the middle of summer was sticky and slow, the kind of heat that clung to you. The cab ride from the airport to his house was familiar enough,—he'd made this trip dozens of times, in offseasons, in the years after his divorce.

But even now, his own house didn't feel like home.

It was a house he bought, not one he built.

Two bedrooms. Nothing fancy. A place to land between baseball seasons.

And right now, it was too quiet.

Jack set his bag down, grabbed a beer from the fridge, and stood in the kitchen, staring at his phone.

Emily was in New York. He knew that. But he hadn't talked to her in months. His daughter was good at avoiding him without actually ignoring him. She answered his calls when she had time, but she didn't go out of her way to make them.

He hit dial.

She picked up on the third ring.

"Dad?"

"Hey, Em," Jack said, shifting the phone to his other ear. "Figured I'd check in while I was home for a few days."

"You're in Nashville?"

"Just for the break. Thought I'd see if you were around."

"Dad, I live in New York."

Jack exhaled. "Yeah. I know. I meant maybe you'd be visiting."

"Not this summer. Too busy."

There was a pause before she added, almost as an afterthought —"How's baseball?"

Jack let out a dry chuckle. "Same as ever."

"You like coaching?"

The way she asked made him think she meant something else.

"Sure," he said, after a beat. "It's baseball."

Emily made a small noise, something between polite and indifferent.

He didn't know what to say next.

Emily did.

"I've gotta go, Dad. I've got work."

Jack nodded, even though she couldn't see him. "Yeah. Of course."

"Take care, okay?"

"You too, kid."

She hung up.

Jack sighed, staring at the phone in his hand.

One down.

Ryan wasn't a phone call away.

Ryan was in Iraq.

Jack had tried writing.

Once.

He still had the draft saved in his email.

Never sent it. Didn't know where to send it.

What the hell was he supposed to say?

"Hey, son. Sorry I wasn't around much when you were growing up. Hope the desert's treating you well."

Yeah. That'd go over great.

He finished his beer and set the empty bottle down on the counter.

For a second, he thought about calling his ex.

Then he thought better of it.

The Braves weren't good this year.

That wasn't news.

Everyone had seen it coming, even if no one had wanted to say it out loud.

The rotation was thin. The bullpen was worse. The offense had flashes of power but no consistency.

They had been hovering under .500 for weeks now, and if the front office wasn't panicking yet, they would be soon.

Jack had been around long enough to know how this worked.

When a team struggles, someone takes the fall.

And it wasn't going to be Bobby Cox.

It was going to be someone like him.

The thought had been sitting in the back of his mind for weeks, but here, in the stillness of a Tennessee night, it finally settled into something heavier.

Would someone hire him again if Atlanta let him go?

He'd been a good coach. Not a great one.

Not memorable.
And in baseball, that mattered.

CHAPTER TWENTY FOUR

She was curious about when the next time the Diamondbacks had a Senior Slugger night.

That's why she had the sports page open on the table.

That's why she was checking their schedule.

And if, in the process, she happened to notice that the Braves would be in town for a weekend series in late July…

Well.

That was just coincidence.

She sat back, tapping her fingers against the desk.

Late July.

Not that far off.

Why did it feel like she was about to do something reckless?

She picked up her phone before she could argue with herself any longer and dialed.

Jack answered on the third ring.

"Maggie," he said, his voice carrying a slight note of surprise. "Wasn't expecting to hear from you."

Maggie swallowed down the flicker of nerves.

"That makes two of us."

Jack chuckled, and it was a warm, easy sound. Familiar, but different.

"What's on your mind?"

Maggie hesitated—just for a second.

Then she said it.

"You're going to be in Phoenix soon."

"You keeping tabs on me?"

"I knew you'd be back at some point."

"And you decided that meant I owed you a meal?"

"I decided it might be nice to catch up properly."

Jack didn't answer right away.

Not in a bad way—more like he was letting the idea settle.

Then, finally—

"Yeah."

Maggie shifting in her chair.

"Sunday night?"

"That works," Jack said. "We've got a day game, so I should be free by early evening."

Maggie tapped her fingers against the desk. "You're flying out that night?"

"No. We're heading to LA on Monday."

"So you won't be in a rush."

"Not unless you pick some place that takes three hours to get a steak," he said dryly.

Maggie smirked. "I'll try to avoid that."

There was a pause, not awkward but noticeable.

Then—

"Maggie?"

"Yeah?"

Jack's voice softened, just slightly.

"I'm glad you called."

She hesitated, just for a second.

Then—"Me too."

And that was as much as she was willing to admit.

"See you then, Jack."

She hung up before she could second-guess herself.

She closed her laptop, turned off the light, and went to bed.

And for the first time in a long time, she wasn't entirely sure what she was walking into.

CHAPTER TWENTY FIVE

The restaurant was quieter than Maggie expected for a Sunday night. The soft hum of conversation filled the dimly lit space, the glow of candlelight flickering against wine glasses. She had arrived a little early—not much, just enough to settle in, order a drink, and take a breath.

She wasn't nervous. At least, that's what she told herself.

This wasn't a date date. It wasn't about rekindling anything. It was just… dinner. A conversation. A chance to see if whatever was still there—whatever had been hovering between them in emails and polite exchanges—was real.

She sipped her wine, glancing at the door.

Jack was late.

Not terribly late, but enough that she checked the time, enough that she wondered if he was going to show at all.

Then—there he was.

And something was wrong.

He wasn't dressed for dinner. He was still in his Braves-issued polo, the team windbreaker slung over his arm. His hair looked like he'd run his hands through it a dozen times. His expression— heavy.

Maggie sat up straighter.

Jack spotted her, gave an obviously fake smile, and walked over. He moved stiffly, like the weight of something had settled on his shoulders.

When he sat down across from her, he didn't say anything for a moment. Just pressed his palms together, stared at the table.

Jack pressed his palms together, staring at the table.

Then—"I got fired."

Maggie blinked. "What?"

Jack let out a slow breath, shaking his head. "They pulled me into a meeting right after the game. Whole staff shake-up. I'm out."

Maggie's stomach twisted.

He wasn't surprised. That much was clear.

But that didn't mean he was okay.

Jack rubbed a hand over his jaw. "I knew it was coming. We've been terrible. Bullpen's a disaster, offense is streaky—this was always how it was gonna go." He let out a humorless laugh. "Still wasn't ready for it."

Maggie opened her mouth, but Jack kept going, words spilling out faster now.

"I'm not even allowed on the team charter flight out of town. That's how this works—you get fired, you're done. No flight back. No gear. Nothing. Just… thanks for your time, clean out your locker." He let out a deep sigh. "Next commercial flight's not until tomorrow morning. They won't literally kick me out of the Marriott for tonight, at least."

Maggie just stared at him.

Jack huffed out a breath, shaking his head. "And you know what the worst part is?"

Maggie didn't answer.

Jack leaned back, rubbing his hands together, jaw tight. "I'm too old for this."

He let the words sit between them for a moment.

"If I was forty-five, I'd be on the phone right now, lining up my next job." His voice was flat, matter-of-fact. "Hell, even fifty, I could swing it. But sixty-three?"

He shook his head. "Nobody's looking for a sixty-three-year-old third base coach who's never been in a front office, never managed. There's nowhere to go."

Maggie felt the weight of those words settle into the space between them.

Jack looked around the room, rubbing his hands over his face. "I've been in baseball since I was twenty-one. I've never done anything else. And now…"

His fingers curled against the tabletop, his voice quieter.

"…I don't know what the hell I'm supposed to do."

Maggie's chest tightened.

She had never seen him like this before.

Jack Riggs had always been in motion. Moving forward, chasing something, always knowing what came next.

And now?

For the first time in his life, he had no next step.

Maggie swallowed.

She had no idea what to say.

She set her glass down. "Eat something."

Jack blinked. "What?"

Maggie nodded toward the menu. "Order something. Drink something. You look like hell."

Jack let out a breath that was almost a laugh, but it didn't reach his eyes.

Still, he reached for the menu.

And for a few minutes, they pretended things were normal.

Maggie asked about the food, Jack picked something without really looking, and the waiter, oblivious to the weight of the moment came and went.

Then, when their drinks were refilled, Maggie leaned forward.

"You don't have to do this alone, Jack."

His eyes flicked up to hers. Something unreadable there.

For a long moment, he didn't say anything.

Then, finally—"I don't even know what 'this' is."

They ate.

Slowly. Quietly. Jack wasn't fully present, and Maggie wasn't going to force him to be.

By the time the check came, he looked exhausted.

And that's when Maggie made the decision.

Jack wasn't going back to the team hotel.

He wasn't flying out until morning.

And she wasn't going to leave him sitting alone in a damn airport

Marriott with nothing but his own thoughts.

Maggie set down her napkin. "Come back to my place."

Jack didn't react at first. Just stared at her.

"Maggie—"

"I'm not suggesting anything." She shook her head. "I just don't think you should be alone right now."

Jack was looking down at and seemingly through the table.

For a moment, she thought he was going to argue.

But then—he just nodded.

The drive was quiet.

Jack barely said a word, and Maggie let the silence settle.

When they got to her house, she led him inside, set her purse down, turned to face him.

Jack ran a hand over his jaw, looking like he still hadn't quite processed all of it.

Maggie nodded toward the couch. "You can take the guest room, but the couch is probably closer to where you'll pass out."

Jack let out a small, tired laugh.

He looked at her. Held her gaze for a moment longer than necessary.

Then—"Thanks, Maggie."

She just nodded.

And when she went to bed that night, she didn't know what tomorrow would bring.

But for the first time, she didn't mind finding out.

CHAPTER TWENTY SIX

Maggie woke to the faint scent of coffee.

For a moment, she forgot.

Forgot that she wasn't alone in the house. Forgot that she'd invited Jack Riggs—fired, exhausted, unmoored Jack Riggs—to stay the night.

Then, as she slipped out of bed and padded toward the kitchen, it all came back.

Jack was standing at the counter, pouring coffee into one of her mismatched mugs. He looked... better. Not good, exactly, but less wrecked than he had last night.

"Didn't take you for an early riser," Maggie murmured.

Jack glanced over, offering a wry grin. "Old habits."

Maggie pulled a mug from the cabinet and joined him, both of them leaning against the counter in silence for a beat.

Jack took a sip, his shoulders easing. "Thanks."

Maggie arched a brow. "For the coffee?"

Jack let out a dry chuckle, shaking his head. "For letting me crash here. For not making a big deal out of it."

Maggie shrugged. "Seemed like you needed a place to land."

Jack tapped his fingers against the mug, gaze distant. "I did."

Silence stretched between them. Not uncomfortable, but... weighted.

Maggie watched him out of the corner of her eye. He wasn't spiraling anymore, but he also wasn't fine.

His whole life had just changed, and he had no idea what came next.

Jack cleared his throat, pushing off the counter. "Cab will be here in a few. I saved you an airport run at least."

Maggie nodded, though she didn't quite want him to leave yet.

They walked to the door together. Jack grabbed the Braves-issued windbreaker he'd tossed over a chair last night but didn't put it on. Instead, he hesitated.

Maggie folded her arms, tilting her head. "What?"

Jack studied her, something unreadable in his expression.

Then—"I'll call you."

Maggie swallowed.

She wasn't sure if he meant it or if he was just saying it because it felt like the right thing to say.

But she nodded anyway.

"Safe flight, Jack."

He lingered just a second longer.

Then—he was gone.

Maggie closed the door, stood there for a long moment.

Then she turned, grabbed her coffee, and exhaled.

Time to figure out what came next.

Maggie sat at her borrowed desk, flipping through another financial report that didn't add up.

The office was quiet. It was late, most of the staff had gone home, but she was still here, surrounded by stacks of files that didn't quite tell the same story as the polished donor brochures in the lobby.

Something was off.

She hadn't been with Phoenix Futures Initiative long—just a few weeks—but already, she could feel it in her gut.

The numbers weren't wrong, exactly. They just weren't right, either.

Money was moving in circles, funds allocated for one program getting re-routed somewhere else. Some vendors PFI supposedly paid didn't seem to exist. And for a nonprofit that prided itself on its "transformational impact," she hadn't seen much actual work being done.

She rubbed her temple, then reached for her coffee—lukewarm

now, half-forgotten.

This was a mess.

And the more she dug, the more she started to think it wasn't just mismanagement.

It was something worse.

Maggie had seen enough and shut the folder.

She wasn't new to corporate nonsense. She'd spent decades cleaning up behind men in suits who promised big and delivered nothing.

She could handle this.

But for the first time, she wasn't sure who she could trust.

The next morning, Maggie walked into Laura Middleton's office and set a folder down on her desk.

She glanced at the file, then back at Maggie. "What's this?"

Maggie folded her arms. "That's what I'd like you to tell me."

Laura gave another laugh, but it was thinner this time. "Oh. Oh, jeez, okay. This is serious, huh?"

She reached for the file, but she was moving slow, like she was stalling. Then, when she finally flipped it open—she immediately shut it again.

Like she could pretend it wasn't there.

Laura stared out up and to the left, shaking her head. "Maggie. Maggie, Maggie, Maggie." She smiled like that was supposed to be disarming. "You ever run a nonprofit before?"

Maggie's eyes narrowed. "I know how business works."

Laura grimaced. "Okay, well, that's not the same thing. Like, *at all*."

She flipped the file open again, flipping too fast through the pages. "Look, I—I get it. I do. The numbers here look, y'know, *funky*, but this isn't a Fortune 500 company. The books aren't as clean, the money moves differently, sometimes there's, um, *discrepancies*—"

Maggie cut in, voice flat. "Missing money."

Laura winced. "Allegedly!"

Maggie stared.

Laura sighed dramatically. "Okay, okay, look. You're—new here, and, uh, there's *context* you don't have yet."

Maggie tilted her head. "Then show me."

Laura exhaled so hard it was almost a whimper.

"Maggie, the priorities just aren't always about, like, *the bottom line.* Our job isn't to maximize profit—it's to do the most good we can with what we have."

Maggie arched a brow. "And that requires paying non-existent vendors?"

Laura visibly panicked. "Oh my God, is that what it looks like?!"

Silence.

Maggie just waited.

Laura groaned, rubbing her forehead. "Look. You're here because you're good at designing org charts and setting up actual HR systems, not auditing spreadsheets. If there's something that needs fixing, I'll—I'll let you know, alright?"

She leaned forward, voice lowering.

"But until then? Maybe just, y'know... *trust that I know what I'm doing.*"

A beat.

Maggie didn't blink.

"That's what I'm trying to figure out."

Laura made a sound that was somewhere between a laugh and a dying animal.

"Oh, for cryin' out loud."

Maggie grabbed the file, tucked it under her arm, and left.

And as she walked back to her desk, she knew one thing for certain.

Laura Middleton was absolutely drowning.

And Maggie wasn't going anywhere until she found out why.

CHAPTER TWENTY SEVEN

The restaurant was loud but comfortable, the kind of place where the margaritas were strong, the chips never stopped coming, and no one cared if you lingered too long. Lynn, already halfway through her second drink, nudged the basket of chips toward Maggie without looking up. Maggie took a sip of her margarita and exhaled, pressing the cool glass against her palm.

"Alright," Brenda said, leaning back in the booth. "You've been weird all night. Spill."

Maggie raised a brow. "Weird?"

Lynn snorted, reaching for a chip. "Oh, definitely weird. You keep zoning out like you're solving the world's biggest mystery. Which means—" she dunked her chip into the salsa, "—you either have a man problem or a work problem."

Brenda smirked. "Or both."

Maggie hesitated.

Brenda's smirk faded. "Oh, shit. It's both, isn't it?"

Maggie sighed, setting her drink down. "I don't even know where to start."

Brenda tilted her head. "Start with the one that won't make me want to drink faster."

Lynn grinned. "Too late, honey. I'm already ahead of you."

Maggie huffed a small laugh, then ran a hand through her hair. "Okay. Work first."

She filled them in—about PFI, about Laura Middleton, about the numbers that didn't make sense. About how things looked fine on the surface but felt wrong underneath.

By the time she was done, Brenda had that assessing, corporate-thinking look in her eyes.

Lynn just whistled. "Damn. And here I thought retirement was supposed to be relaxing."

Brenda tapped her fingers against the table. "You think they're actually cooking the books, or just playing fast and loose with the rules?"

Maggie exhaled. "I don't know yet. But Laura's too smooth about it. Either she's done this before, or she's real good at pretending she hasn't."

Brenda nodded slowly. "And what's your move?"

Maggie hesitated, then shrugged. "I dig deeper."

Brenda sighed, rubbing her temple. "Of course you do."

Lynn reached for another chip. "Look, I'm just saying—if this turns into some kind of true crime documentary, I want to be the fun best friend in all the interviews."

Maggie rolled her eyes.

Brenda, on the other hand, wasn't laughing. "Be careful with this, Mags."

Maggie met her gaze. "I will."

But they both knew she wasn't walking away.

Brenda leaned forward, folding her arms. "Alright. That's the work disaster. Now tell me why you also look like a woman who's walked headfirst into a bad idea with a man."

Maggie sighed.

Lynn's eyes lit up. "Wait, is this about your mystery man from the steakhouse?"

Brenda turned sharply. "What steakhouse?"

Maggie groaned. "You two are relentless."

Brenda frowned. "No, no. You don't get to hold out on me. What steakhouse?"

Lynn grinned. "A couple months ago, we're at dinner, and Maggie sees this guy across the restaurant—freezes like she's seen a ghost."

Brenda's eyes narrowed. "And you're just now telling me this?"

Lynn shrugged. "I was waiting for her to spill. I didn't know it was going to take this long."

Brenda turned back to Maggie. "Who was it?"

Maggie pressed her lips together, then exhaled. "Jack Riggs."

Silence.

Then—Brenda blinked. "Wait. Your Jack Riggs?"

Lynn's brows shot up. "Baseball Jack? The ex?"

Maggie rubbed her temples. "Yes. And yes."

Brenda let out a slow whistle. "Damn, Maggie. That's..." she trailed off.

Maggie sighed. "A bad idea?"

Brenda tilted her head. "Not what I was going to say."

Lynn, however, had no such hesitation. "Oh, it's a bad idea. But that doesn't mean you're not gonna do it."

Maggie huffed a small laugh.

Brenda frowned. "So... what's happening there? You're back in touch?"

Maggie nodded slowly. "Yeah. And it's... weird. Familiar but not. He got fired last week, and he's—" she hesitated, searching for the words. "Lost."

Brenda's expression softened. "And you're worried about him."

Maggie nodded.

Lynn popped a chip into her mouth. "I mean, at least he's not an arrogant pilot."

Brenda snorted. "No kidding."

Maggie shook her head. "He's still Jack. Just... older. And a little broken."

Brenda studied her. "And you?"

Maggie frowned. "What about me?"

Brenda tilted her head. "Are you just worried about him, or are you thinking about picking this back up?"

Maggie hesitated.

Brenda caught it immediately.

"Mags."

Maggie sighed, reaching for her margarita. "I don't know."

Brenda gave her a look. "You've never been great at 'I don't know.'"

Maggie just took a sip. "Well, there's a first time for everything."

Brenda didn't press.

Lynn just grinned. "This is gonna be fun to watch."

Maggie shook her head. "You two are the worst."

Lynn lifted her glass. "We love you too, babe."

CHAPTER TWENTY EIGHT

The drive to Vanderbilt felt different this time.

Jack had made this trip plenty of times before—recruiting visits, alumni events, the occasional charity banquet where they dragged out the old players for a wave and a handshake. He knew the route from the airport like the back of his hand, could probably drive it blind if he had to.

But today, there was no banquet. No fundraiser. No pretense.

Today, he was here for himself.

The thought made his stomach twist.

Jack exhaled, adjusting his grip on the wheel as he passed the familiar green road sign:

Vanderbilt University – 2 miles

The city had changed since he was a kid here. The skyline had stretched taller, the traffic had thickened, and the old brick buildings he remembered had been renovated or replaced with something sleeker, newer. But this stretch of road—the one leading onto campus—still felt the same.

As he merged onto West End Avenue, the university came into view, its signature red-brick facades peeking through the spring-green canopy of trees. The sight of it made something pull tight in his chest.

This had been home once.

He hadn't thought about it that way in a long time.

Jack rolled his shoulders, trying to shake the feeling. He wasn't here for nostalgia. He was here for a job.

Or at least, to find out if there was one.

He had made the call two days ago.

To his surprise, Coach Reilly had picked up on the first ring.

"Jack Riggs," Reilly had said, his voice warm, familiar. "I'd say this is a surprise, but it's not. Figured I'd hear from you sooner or later."

Jack had chuckled, though there wasn't much humor in it. "Guess I'm that predictable."

Reilly hadn't denied it.

They'd played together for a few years back in the seventies—Reilly as a backup catcher, Jack still hanging onto an outfield spot. They hadn't been close, exactly, but they'd gotten along. Kept in touch here and there over the years, mostly through alumni events or the occasional email about some player they both knew.

When Jack told him why he was calling, Reilly hadn't hesitated.

"Come on by," he had said. "We'll talk."

Jack had appreciated the lack of fanfare.

Now, as he pulled into the parking lot outside the baseball facility, he wasn't sure if that was a good thing or a bad thing. Reilly met him at the door, all easy grins and sturdy handshakes.

The man had aged well—grayer than Jack remembered, maybe a little softer around the middle, but still with that sharp, assessing look in his eyes. The kind of look only a catcher had, like he was always sizing up a pitcher, waiting to call the next play.

"Riggs," he said, clapping Jack on the back. "Hell of a thing, seeing you walk in here again."

Jack smirked. "Yeah, well. Didn't expect to be back under these circumstances."

Reilly huffed a laugh. "Funny how life works."

They walked through the facility, passing framed photos of championship teams, jerseys from alumni who had gone on to the majors. Jack's wasn't up there. He had played pro ball, sure, but he'd never been *that* guy. Never the one they pointed to when they talked about Vanderbilt's greatest.

That was fine.

He wasn't here to be remembered. He was here to find a job.

Reilly led him into his office, a modest space with shelves stacked with scouting reports and old game balls. The air smelled like fresh-cut grass and leather—baseball through and through.

Jack took a seat.

Reilly leaned back in his chair. "So," he said, "what's on your mind?"

No sense in dancing around it.

"You know what happened with Atlanta."

Reilly nodded.

"I need to figure out what's next," Jack continued. "I don't know if coaching college ball is the right fit, but... I wanted to see what was out there."

Reilly studied him for a long moment, arms folded across his chest.

Jack knew that look.

It was the same look he used to give young guys who thought they were ready for the big leagues before they really were.

"You sure about this?" Reilly asked finally. "College ball's a different animal, Riggs. It ain't just about the game. You gotta recruit. You gotta babysit. These kids aren't pros yet."

Jack shrugged. "I've been around rookies. Spent years coaching twenty-year-olds who think they know everything. How different can it be?"

Reilly smirked. "You'd be surprised."

Jack didn't say anything.

Reilly let out a slow breath, tapping a pen against his desk.

"Look," he said. "I respect the hell out of you, Jack. Always have. And if we had something open, I'd fight to bring you on. But right now? There's nothing."

Jack had been expecting it.

Didn't make it easier to hear.

"Nothing at all?" he asked, even though he already knew the answer.

Reilly shook his head. "Not unless you want to start at the bottom. Volunteer work. Maybe a grad assistant spot, but..." He trailed off, giving Jack a pointed look.

Jack understood.

He wasn't some fresh-out-of-school kid trying to break into

coaching. He wasn't about to spend his days hauling gear and running drills for free.

That wasn't why he was here.

Reilly sighed, rubbing a hand over his jaw. "If something opens up, I'll call you. You know that."

Jack nodded. "Yeah. I appreciate it."

Reilly hesitated, then leaned forward.

"Can I give you some advice?"

Jack smirked. "Like I could stop you."

Reilly chuckled, shaking his head. Then, his expression turned serious.

"Maybe it's time to stop looking for what's next in baseball."

Jack tensed.

Reilly saw it.

"I'm not saying you can't coach," he added quickly. "Hell, you'd be a damn good one. But you've been in this game for forty years. Maybe it's time to figure out what life looks like without it."

Jack exhaled through his nose. "And what if I don't want to?"

Reilly shrugged. "Then you'll keep chasing it. And maybe you'll find something. But if you don't?" He spread his hands. "You gotta be ready for that too."

Jack didn't answer.

Because he wasn't sure he was.

Reilly leaned back, giving him a long, assessing look.

Then he smirked. "And if you *do* want to coach? You ever think about teaching the game to kids who *need* it?"

Jack frowned. "What do you mean?"

"There's a program in Atlanta. Helps underprivileged kids get into baseball. Teaches them the fundamentals, gives them a shot at scholarships. They're always looking for good people."

Jack hesitated.

That wasn't what he'd been thinking about.

That wasn't the kind of coaching he had pictured.

Reilly must've seen the doubt on his face, because he grinned. "I know, I know. You're not a Little League guy. But think about it."

Jack nodded, but he wasn't sure he would.

They shook hands, and Jack walked out of the office, through the hallways lined with pictures of teams he had once been a part of.

He stepped outside, the warm spring air hitting him full force.

For a long moment, he just stood there.

Then, finally, he let out a slow breath, pulled out his keys, and walked to his car.

Time to figure out what the hell came next.

~~~~~~~~~~

Jack sat at the kitchen table, staring at the half-empty coffee cup in front of him, his fingers drumming lightly against the ceramic. He'd been in town for three weeks, and he already felt both restless and stuck at the same time.

He had been here long enough to shake hands, long enough to confirm that there was no place for him at Vanderbilt, long enough to hear the polite variations of *We'd love to have you, but there's just no room right now.*

Long enough to realize that no one was dying for him to walk through their door.

It wasn't that he was surprised. He'd known, deep down, that baseball had been inching away from him for years. That the game didn't need him the way he needed it.

But knowing it and *feeling it* were two different things.

His phone buzzed against the table.

Jack frowned, glancing at the screen.

Maggie Callahan.

He hesitated.

They hadn't talked much since he left Phoenix. They hadn't *not* talked, either—it was just that neither of them had really reached out. The space had settled between them naturally, the kind of quiet that wasn't exactly bad but wasn't exactly good, either.

Jack picked up the phone, pressing it to his ear.

"Maggie."

There was a pause. Then—

"You ever hear the name Dylan Sheridan?"

Jack went still.

For a second, he wasn't in his kitchen.

He was thirty-one years old, sitting on a clubhouse bench in Milwaukee, watching a twenty-year-old rich kid saunter around like he owned the place—because, in a way, he did.

His grip tightened around the phone.

"Yeah," he said slowly. "I know him."

Maggie exhaled, and Jack could hear her moving, like she was pacing.

"I thought you might," she said. "His name popped up in the Phoenix Futures Initiative stuff."

Jack closed his eyes.

Of course it did.

"What's he tied to?" he asked.

"Funding, mostly," Maggie said. "Big money. His name's attached to some of their biggest donors, but there's barely a paper trail. Like someone doesn't want his connection to be too obvious."

Jack let out a slow breath, rolling his shoulders.

"Yeah," he muttered. "That sounds like Dylan."

The guy had been a snake from the moment he slithered into baseball.

Jack had played for Milwaukee in the early '70s, back when Dylan Sheridan was just another owner's son who liked to act like he was in charge. He wasn't even in college yet, but he ran around the clubhouse like he was a damn GM, dropping his last name like a hammer, making himself comfortable in places he didn't belong.

And the worst part?

His father let him.

Frank Sheridan had owned the Brewers, but he had never *loved* baseball. He loved money. He loved power. And he loved the idea of his son carrying on the family legacy—even if Dylan was too arrogant, too reckless, too entitled to ever *earn* his place in the sport.

Jack had watched Dylan ruin things just because he *could.*

Watched him flash money at guys who were barely making league minimum, promising them favors he had no business promising.

Watched him slip into the front office, sweet-talking his way into conversations he didn't belong in.

Watched him *gamble*, not just with money, but with people.

There had been rumors—always rumors.

Dylan betting on things he shouldn't.

Dylan throwing money around where it didn't belong.

Dylan sticking his nose in trade discussions, trying to play kingmaker.

Jack had never trusted him.

And now Dylan was wrapped up in PFI?

Jack sucked air through his teeth, dragging a hand down his face.

"Mags," he said. "You need to be careful with this guy."

"I know," Maggie said. "That's why I called you."

Jack's jaw clenched.

He hadn't expected to feel this angry about it. It had been *decades* since he'd even thought about the Sheridans, but hearing that name now—knowing Dylan had sunk his claws into something new—made his blood run hot.

"You said there's no real paper trail?" Jack asked.

"Nothing direct," Maggie said. "But I know he's involved. I just don't have the proof yet."

Jack sighed, leaning back in his chair.

"He's smart enough to cover his tracks," he said. "At least, on the surface. But there's no way in hell he's clean. The guy's a walking scandal waiting to happen."

Maggie was quiet for a beat.

Then—

"What do you remember about him?"

Jack smirked, but there was no humor in it.

"That he's a piece of shit."

Maggie let out a breath that sounded suspiciously like a laugh.

"Helpful," she said dryly.

Jack shook his head, rubbing a hand over his jaw.

"I remember him being reckless," he said. "Cocky. Thought he was untouchable because his dad owned the team. He never had to work for anything. And he *liked* screwing with people. Especially if they were desperate."

Maggie hummed thoughtfully.

"That tracks," she said. "PFI deals with people who are desperate. It's supposed to help people get back on their feet, but if the wrong people are running things…" She trailed off.

Jack knew exactly what she meant.

"If Sheridan's involved," he said, "then someone's getting screwed over."

Maggie sighed. "I think you're right."

Another pause.

Then—

"I need your help, Jack."

He knew what she was asking.

He could feel the weight of it pressing down on him already.

For weeks, he had been floating. No job, no direction, nothing solid to grab onto.

And now, Maggie was handing him something real.

Something worth fighting for.

Jack ran a hand over his face, then smirked, shaking his head.

"Yeah, Mags," he said, voice rough. "I'm in."

Maggie didn't thank him. Didn't have to.

She just said, "I'll send you what I have."

Jack nodded, even though she couldn't see him.

"Good," he said. "And Maggie?"

"Yeah?"

"If Sheridan's involved, you're going to want more than just paperwork. You're going to need people who can talk."

Maggie was silent for a second.

Then—

"You know someone?"

Jack smirked.

"Oh, I know a few."

And just like that, Jack Riggs had a reason to stay in the game.

CHAPTER TWENTY NINE

Dylan Sheridan had always been careful, but careful only went so far when you spent your whole life assuming rules didn't apply to you. Somewhere out there, someone knew something real. Someone had a story about Sheridan that wasn't just locker room whispers and bad gut feelings.

Jack just had to find the right guy.

He started jotting names down.

People Who Might Talk

1. **Old Brewers teammates** – Guys who were around back when Dylan was screwing with the team. Problem was, most of them had moved on. Some were coaching, some were front-office guys, some were **too deep in baseball politics to stick their necks out now.**

2. **Front-office guys from back in the day** – If anyone had real dirt on the Sheridans, it'd be someone who worked upstairs. But Frank Sheridan had owned the team **thirty years ago.** Anyone who had been under him was either retired, dead, or too old to care.

3. **Players Dylan had 'helped'** – This was the one that stuck in Jack's head the longest.

Dylan had liked messing with players.

Guys who were young, desperate, on the edge of getting cut. The kind of guys who wouldn't say no if the owner's kid offered them a little something extra to stay on the roster.

Jack had seen it firsthand—Dylan hanging around the younger guys, buying them drinks, offering favors that always came with strings attached.

And the ones who took those deals? They either made it, barely, or they disappeared fast.

Jack tapped the pen against his notepad, thinking.

Who was the last guy he remembered Dylan screwing over?

Then it hit him.

Keith Holloway.

He had been a talented outfielder, good hands, decent speed, but never quite a superstar. Drafted by the Brewers in '89, played a few seasons, then gone.

Jack still remembered the whispers.

Holloway had a gambling problem.

He had been running up debts all over town, and word around the clubhouse was Dylan helped him out. Paid off some of his debts. Even got him another year on the roster.

Then, suddenly, Holloway was out of baseball completely.

No official scandal. No big media blow-up.

Just… vanished.

Jack grabbed his phone, flipped through his contacts. No Keith Holloway, of course. It had been too long. But that didn't mean he couldn't track him down.

He called Maggie, She answered immediately.

"You ever run background checks on people?"

"I've been involved in the hirings of thousands of people. There's things we would need to know. Thinking of someone?"

"Keith Holloway. Brewers, late '80s. See if he's still around."

"On it. Thanks."

Jack smiled and leaned back against the couch.

For the first time in weeks, he felt like he was doing something that mattered.

CHAPTER THIRTY

Maggie sat at her kitchen table, eyes locked on her laptop screen, fingers skimming across the keyboard. She was deep in the kind of research rabbit hole that made time blur, the kind where one click led to another, each link pulling her further into something she hadn't even realized she was chasing.

Keith Holloway.

She wasn't sure why the name had stuck with her the way it did. Maybe it was the way Jack had said it—like it meant something. Like it had weight.

And if Jack thought it was important, then Maggie wasn't about to let it go.

She leaned forward, scanning the old player stats and scattered newspaper mentions.

Holloway had been drafted in '89, played a few years for the Brewers, then vanished. No major injury, no official scandal. Just... gone.

She kept searching.

A few scattered references popped up—mentions of him playing in Puerto Rico for a season, a coaching stint at a high school in Ohio. But then, radio silence for nearly two decades.

Until she found something buried in public court records from three years ago.

Keith Holloway – Defendant.

Her pulse kicked up.

She clicked on the link, eyes scanning the document.

Fraud charges.

Something about shady loan deals, an investment scam. Case dismissed.

Maggie frowned. That didn't make sense.

Keith Holloway had been a ballplayer. Not a businessman. Not some investment guru. So what the hell was he doing wrapped up in financial fraud?

She dug deeper, pulling up everything she could on the case.

Most of the documents were sealed, but she found an address linked to the court filing.

Maggie clicked. Scanned. Then stopped cold.

Last known address: Tucson, Arizona.

Her breath caught.

Tucson.

Two hours south of Phoenix.

Her fingers hovered over the keyboard. Jack was in Nashville. But Holloway—Holloway was practically in their backyard.

She didn't know what it meant yet, but she knew one thing: Jack needed to know.

Jack was halfway through a whiskey he wasn't enjoying when his phone lit up.

Maggie.

He frowned, setting the glass down and answering.

"Callahan."

"You sitting down?" she asked, voice brisk.

Jack laughed, running a hand over his jaw. "Should I be?"

"Keith Holloway's in Tucson."

Jack's grip on the phone tightened.

"Come again?"

"Last known address," Maggie said. "Court records. Three years ago, he got tied up in a fraud case. Case got dismissed, but his last address on record is Tucson."

Jack let out a sharp breath, sitting up in his chair. Tucson.

Holloway was in Arizona! Still close enough to be involved in something.

"Jesus," he muttered.

Maggie didn't say anything for a second, then—soft, careful, but knowing—

"You were gonna come back eventually, weren't you?"

Jack exhaled through his nose, shaking his head. "You sound awful damn sure about that."

"I am."

Jack smirked despite himself.

Maggie's voice turned serious again.

"You said Holloway might know something about Sheridan. If he's in Tucson, we need to find him."

Jack scrubbed a hand down his face. Hell.

He'd been trying to figure out his next move, and now the decision was made for him.

No job, no plan, no idea what the hell he was doing—but he knew one thing:

It was time to go back to Phoenix.

Jack sighed, already pulling up flights.

"Mags?"

"Yeah?"

"I'll be there tomorrow."

CHAPTER THIRTY ONE

The desert stretched out endless on either side of the highway, the sky just starting to soften into gold and lavender as the sun dipped lower.

Maggie had been driving for an hour, Jack in the passenger seat, the radio playing soft, forgettable classic rock.

They'd started out talking about Holloway, Sheridan, the logistics of the trip. But after a while, the conversation had fizzled into quiet.

And now?

Now Jack was watching her.

Not in the casual, passing way he used to, when they worked together and the feelings were complicated and ignorable.

Now, it was different.

She felt it too.

The weight of his gaze. The way the silence wasn't really silence.

Maggie cleared her throat, adjusting her grip on the wheel. "You're staring."

Jack smirked. "Observing."

Maggie huffed. "And what, exactly, are you *observing*?"

Jack shrugged, voice lazy. "Just trying to remember the last time we were in a car together this long without trying to jump each other."

Maggie let out a short laugh. "That would be never."

Jack grinned, but didn't argue.

They lapsed back into silence, but this time it was different.

A little looser.

A little easier.

Jack scratched his chin and resettled in his seat. "Ever think about it?"

Maggie frowned. "Think about what?"

Jack turned his head toward her, studying her profile.

"Back then. Why we didn't work."

Maggie's fingers tensed slightly on the wheel.

She didn't answer right away.

Jack just watched her, waiting.

Finally, Maggie exhaled. "We were never in the same place. Not really."

Jack tipped his head slightly. "What do you mean?"

Maggie hesitated. Then—honest, but not unkind—"You were still chasing baseball. And I was never gonna be the girl who waited around."

Jack was quiet for a long beat.

Maggie didn't fill the silence.

Then—softer this time—Jack murmured, "You wouldn't have waited if I asked?"

Maggie's chest tightened.

That wasn't fair.

She found herself shaking her head. "Would you have given it up if I asked?"

Jack didn't move. Didn't speak.

And there it was.

The thing neither of them ever said out loud.

Maggie swallowed. "It wasn't a choice, Jack. It was just—*who we were then.*"

Jack turned his head, looking out the window.

The sky was darker now. The road empty, stretching on ahead of them.

Finally, he said, "And now?"

Maggie's fingers flexed slightly on the wheel.

Now.

Now, she didn't know.

She kept her eyes on the road, pulse a little unsteady.

Jack's voice was quieter this time.

"You ever wonder if we would've worked if we met at a different

time?"
Maggie licked her lips, fingers gripping the wheel tighter.
She let out a soft, almost-laugh.
"Jack."
Jack smirked. "What?"
Maggie shook her head. "You're supposed to be the guy who never looks back."
Jack watched her, serious now. "Maybe I'm getting old."
Maggie's stomach fluttered.
She didn't look at him.
Didn't say anything.
But she felt the shift.
The space between them was smaller now.
Not physically.
But in every other way that mattered.

CHAPTER THIRTY TWO

The complex was exactly what they expected. Low-income, sun-bleached, with patches of stucco missing from the exterior walls. The kind of place where people minded their own business.

Jack and Maggie walked up the second-floor balcony, stopping outside Apartment 206. Jack knocked, firm but not aggressive.

No answer.

He knocked again.

From inside, footsteps.

Then the door cracked open, and there he was—Keith Holloway.

Jack barely recognized him. Thinner, older, worn down. But those eyes? Same as ever—sharp, a little suspicious, like he was always waiting for the next bad thing to hit.

He looked at Jack, then at Maggie and the stack of documents in her hands, then back at Jack.

"Shit," Keith muttered. "This can't be good."

Jack smirked. "Nice to see you too, Holloway."

Keith exhaled, stepping back and opening the door wider. "Come in. But make it quick."

The place was sparse. A couch, a small TV, stacks of unopened mail on the counter. No photos, no signs of family.

Keith sank into an old recliner, rubbing a hand over his face.

Jack leaned against the counter while Maggie stayed standing, arms crossed, taking everything in.

Keith sighed. "So. What's this about?"

Jack didn't dance around it. "Dylan Sheridan."

Keith flinched. Just barely. But it was there.

Jack saw Maggie catch it, too.

Keith let out a long breath. "Damn. Figured someone would come knocking eventually."

Maggie spoke up. "We know he's been using PFI to launder money. What we don't have is proof."

Keith gave a humorless chuckle. "Yeah, well. You're not gonna find a receipt that says 'Dylan Sheridan's Fraud Fund.' Guy's smarter than that."

Jack kept his eyes on him. "But you've got something, don't you?"

Keith hesitated.

Then he nodded. "Yeah. I do."

Maggie blinked, clearly surprised by how easy that was.

Jack just smirked.

Keith pushed himself up from the chair and walked over to a small metal filing cabinet. He yanked open a drawer, dug around for a minute, then pulled out a thick folder.

"Kept this for insurance," Keith muttered, tossing it onto the table. "Didn't think I'd ever actually use it."

Maggie was already flipping through it, her eyes scanning the documents. Bank records, wire transfers, suspicious donations.

Jack watched her. He knew that look. She was locked in.

"This is it," she murmured.

"It's enough to sink him?" Jack questioned.

Maggie nodded. "Yeah. It's enough."

For a second, none of them said anything.

Then Keith snorted. "Well. Guess that's that."

Jack studied him. "What happens to you now?"

Keith gave a half-shrug. "Hell if I know. Not like I've got much left to lose."

Jack didn't buy that. Keith was beaten down, but not broken.

Maybe this was the start of something better for him, too.

"Appreciate it, Holloway," Jack said.

Keith just huffed. "Yeah, yeah. Just don't get me killed."

Maggie smirked. "Not our style."

And with that, they had everything they needed.

Jack and Maggie didn't talk much for the first stretch of the drive back.

But it wasn't silence.

It was something else.

Something settled.

Maggie had the folder in her lap, fingers running over the edges. She wasn't looking at the documents anymore—just thinking.

Jack glanced over at her. "Feels different now, doesn't it?"

She looked up, brow raised.

Jack nodded toward the folder. "You're not chasing a lead anymore. You're holding the whole damn thing."

Maggie exhaled, leaning back against the headrest. "Yeah."

Jack smirked, eyes back on the road. "Told you we'd get him."

Maggie watched him for a second, then shook her head, smiling. "Yeah," she murmured. "You did."

The tension between them had shifted.

It wasn't just the rush of an investigation anymore.

It was something else—something bigger.

Maggie stretched out her legs, letting out a slow breath. "We should celebrate."

Jack smirked. "You suggesting a bottle of tequila and some bad decisions?"

Maggie snorted. "No. I was thinking something *civilized*."

Jack sighed dramatically. "Shame."

She rolled her eyes but didn't stop smirking.

Jack felt it, that pull between them—undeniable now, impossible to ignore.

And for the first time in a long time, he wasn't running from it.

CHAPTER THIRTY THREE

Maggie had forgotten what her house looked like without a layer of dust and construction materials covering everything.

Now, finally, it was finished.

The fresh paint, the refinished floors, the new kitchen—it all looked good, felt good, but more than that, it finally felt like hers.

And for the first time in weeks, she wasn't buried in investigative work or late-night phone calls or tracking down sources in Tucson. Tonight, it was just her, Brenda, and Lynn, takeout containers scattered across the kitchen island, and an open bottle of wine.

Lynn held up her glass. "To Maggie, the only woman crazy enough to renovate a house and take down a corrupt nonprofit at the same time."

Brenda clinked her glass against hers. "And somehow survive both."

Maggie rolled her eyes but lifted her glass anyway. "I'll drink to that."

The wine was cold and crisp, and when she set her glass down, she let out a long, happy, sigh.

"You look different," Brenda said, studying her.

Maggie frowned. "Different how?"

Brenda shrugged. "Lighter. Like you're not carrying everything by yourself anymore."

Maggie blinked. She hadn't really thought about it, but... yeah. Maybe she did feel lighter.

She'd spent so much time fighting alone. For stories, for her career, for people to take her seriously.

Now, with the PFI story on the verge of breaking, and with Jack—Jack, who had come back with her to Phoenix, who hadn't run the second it was over—it was different.

Lynn plopped down onto the barstool, kicking off her shoes. "So what's the next move? You're gonna take this straight to the press?"

Maggie hesitated. "Yeah. I have everything I need. But I have to be smart about it. If I take it to the wrong outlet, Sheridan spins it before it even lands."

Brenda nodded. "You need someone solid. Someone who won't let him bury the story."

Lynn took a sip of wine, then tilted her head. "You should talk to Eli."

Maggie frowned. "Who's Eli?"

Lynn and Brenda exchanged a look.

"My ex," Lynn said, smirking. "Investigative journalist. Good one. He's worked on sports finance cases before. If you want this thing to hit the right way, you need him."

Maggie narrowed her eyes. "And you're just telling me this now?"

Lynn shrugged, entirely unbothered. "We were celebrating your house first. Priorities."

Brenda snorted. "She's not wrong."

Maggie just shook her head, already pulling up her phone.

"Fine," she muttered. "Give me his number."

Lynn grinned and rattled it off.

And just like that, the last piece slid into place.

CHAPTER THIRTY FOUR

He hadn't planned on sticking around Phoenix.

At least, that's what he told himself.

But after Tucson, after Holloway, after watching Maggie put the final piece of the puzzle together, he hadn't booked a flight back to Nashville. Hadn't even thought about it.

Instead, he made one call.

"You still got that place in Tempe?"

"Yeah," the guy had said, like it wasn't even a question. "I only use it for spring training. Stay as long as you need."

The guy—a former All-Star Jack had coached in Atlanta—had always been a little too loose with money. Hadn't made Jack's mistakes exactly, but close. Big contracts, big spending, a condo he barely remembered owning.

Jack had seen it before. Had been there before.

So now, instead of crashing on a buddy's couch or renting a motel, he had a place in Phoenix.

And really, nowhere else to be.

He had spent half his life in places like this.

Chain-link batting cages, worn-down rubber mats, the sound of aluminum cracking against leather. The smell of sweat and dust mixing under the harsh glow of overhead lights.

It wasn't the kind of place pros trained. It was where kids with big dreams and no money came to take their hacks.

Which, at the moment, described the three teenagers a few stalls down—all raw talent and terrible mechanics, swinging like they were trying to murder the ball instead of hit it.

Jack ignored them at first, rolling his shoulders, settling into the easy rhythm of getting his own reps in.

He hadn't taken a real swing in years. Coaching had been about mechanics, not muscle memory. But something about tonight— about feeling like he was standing at the edge of something again, but not quite stepping forward—made him want to just hit.

The first ball came in at 60 mph, slow compared to what he was used to, but fast enough to feel real.

He swung.

Crack.

The bat connected clean. A sharp, tight line drive.

Jack eyed the pitching machine.

He took another swing. Then another. And another.

Jack had been so lost in his own head that he didn't notice one of the teenagers watching him until the kid cleared his throat.

"Uh, hey."

Jack turned, still gripping the bat.

The kid—sixteen, maybe seventeen—looked a little nervous, holding his own bat like he wasn't quite sure what to do with it.

Jack frowned. "Yeah?"

The kid hesitated, then motioned toward Jack's stall.

"You, uh… you play college ball or something?"

Jack huffed out a quiet laugh. College ball. Christ.

"Something like that," he said, shaking his head.

The kid scratched the back of his head. "Could you show me how to—" He stopped, embarrassed. "I mean, if you've got time."

Jack looked at him.

Then, slowly, he stepped out of his cage, tapping the bat against his palm.

"Lemme see your stance."

The kid brightened immediately, gripping his bat, getting into a god-awful position.

Jack laughed inside his head. This was gonna take a minute.

But for the first time in weeks, he wasn't thinking about what came next.

He was just here.
Doing what he knew how to do.
And for once, that felt like enough.

CHAPTER THIRTY FIVE

Jack didn't love journalists.

Nothing personal—just years of dealing with reporters who cared more about a headline than the truth. Some of them were fine, but most? Most were vultures. They'd circle a guy at his worst moment, scribbling down whatever version of the story got the most clicks.

So when Maggie told him they were meeting a reporter, he wasn't exactly thrilled.

But he went anyway.

Because this wasn't just about him.

And because Maggie had that look in her eye. The one that said we're doing this, so shut up and get on board.

So he did.

They met in a quiet corner of a coffee shop in downtown Phoenix. Jack sat across from Maggie, arms crossed, waiting.

Then Eli walked in.

He was younger than Jack expected—early 40s, sharp brown eyes, a little wiry, like a guy who ran on caffeine and adrenaline. He had the kind of energy Jack didn't trust—the kind that made a guy look too interested, too sharp, like he was already writing the story in his head before you even opened your mouth.

Jack didn't like it.

Maggie, though?

She sat back, cool and collected, like she'd done this a hundred times before.

"Carter," she said, giving him a nod.

"Maggie." He nodded back, dropping into the seat across from them. He glanced at Jack, then at her again. "This him?"

Jack arched a brow. "Him" who?

Maggie smirked. "Jack Riggs. He's the reason we found Holloway."

Eli gave him a quick once-over. "The baseball guy."

Jack didn't blink. "The journalist guy."

Maggie sighed. "Jesus. Can we skip the pissing contest?"

Eli grinned, unbothered. "Yeah, yeah. Let's see what you've got."

Maggie slid the Holloway file across the table.

Eli flipped it open, his gaze sharpening as he scanned the documents. Bank records. Wire transfers. Suspicious donations.

Jack watched him read, watched his expression shift from curiosity to something else.

By the time he reached the last page, Eli let out a low whistle.

"Damn," he muttered. He leaned back in his chair, tapping a finger against the file. "This is real."

Jack smirked. "No shit."

Eli ignored him, still flipping through the pages.

"Sheridan's been untouchable for years," he said. "Rumors, speculation, but nothing concrete. If this checks out—and it will—this could bury him."

Maggie nodded. "That's the idea."

Eli spoke as he still absorbed what he'd just reviewed. "This is gonna take a minute to verify, but if it holds up? We're looking at fraud, financial crimes, tax evasion at the very least. Could be bigger."

Jack crossed his arms. "So what happens next?"

Eli tapped the folder. "I start making calls. Digging into the nonprofit angle, cross-checking the names here with the PFI board and donors. Once it's airtight, I publish."

Maggie leaned forward. "How long?"

Eli hesitated. "A week or two, probably."

Jack frowned. "A week?"

Eli looked at him. "I'm sure you went a week without a hit, how long is that really?"

Jack clenched his jaw but didn't argue with the guy.

Maggie watched him for a second, then turned back to Eli. "Alright. Do what you need to do."

Eli gave her a short nod. Then, for the first time, he actually looked at her.

"You know, this could make your career."

Maggie smirked. "Or burn it to the ground."

Eli chuckled. "Yeah. That too."

He grabbed the folder, tucked it into his bag, then stood. "I'll be in touch."

Jack didn't watch him go. Just mumbled something to himself.

Maggie arched a brow. "You gonna glare at him every time we see him?"

Jack shrugged. "Ask me after he prints the damn story."

Maggie shook her head, amused. "You're impossible."

Jack just smirked.

And with that, the story was officially out of their hands.

CHAPTER THIRTY SIX

The story broke on a Monday morning.

EXCLUSIVE: Former MLB Owner's Son Tied to Charity Finance Scandal

by Eli Carter, The Arizona Republic

The article laid it all out—Holloway's documents, the financial inconsistencies, the donations funneled through shell accounts, the PFI connection. It was airtight.

And at the center of it all? Dylan Sheridan.

Sheridan's lawyers had already put out a statement calling the allegations "baseless and defamatory." But it didn't matter. The public didn't buy it.

By noon, major news outlets had picked it up.

By mid-afternoon, sponsors were pulling funding.

By nightfall, Sheridan had resigned from the PFI board.

Maggie called around nine.

"Tell me you're seeing this," she said.

Jack smirked. "Seeing it. Reading it. Thinking about framing it."

Maggie let out a breath that sounded half-relieved, half-exhausted. "It's happening."

"Yeah," Jack said. "It is."

For a second, neither of them spoke.

Then—softer—Maggie said, "I didn't think it would feel like this."

Jack leaned back against the couch. "Like what?"

"Like... I thought I'd feel done. But I don't."

Jack knew that feeling.

Knew what it was like to climb the mountain, only to realize the summit wasn't the end.

He ran a hand through his hair. "So what now?"

Maggie was quiet for a moment. Then—

"The PFI board called me."

Jack straightened. "Yeah?"

"They want me to take over. Executive Director."

Jack let out a low whistle. Not bad for a gal who started this thing by accident.

"You gonna do it?"

Maggie exhaled. "I think I have to."

Jack smirked. "Not exactly a ringing endorsement."

Maggie huffed out a laugh, but when she spoke again, her voice was steady. "I want to fix it. The organization means something. Just because Sheridan used it to line his pockets doesn't mean it wasn't doing real good."

Jack nodded, even though she couldn't see him. "Then fix it."

Maggie went quiet again.

Then, finally, she said, "I want you to stay."

Jack's breath caught.

She didn't mean help her run PFI. She meant stay in Phoenix. Stay with her.

He closed his eyes, exhaled slow. "Mags..."

"No pressure," she said quickly. "I just—I don't think you have to run this time."

Jack swallowed.

He wasn't running.

Not anymore.

CHAPTER THIRTY SEVEN

Jack adjusted the cuffs of his only decent dress shirt, shifting against the heat that had settled in the air just after sunset.

They stepped out of the Arizona Attorney General's office, walking toward a quiet stretch of downtown, the last of the day's light fading against the skyline.

Ahead, the restaurant came into view—a small, unassuming place tucked into the shadow of Chase Field.

The ballpark loomed just down the street, its massive structure stretching toward the sky, dark and empty. The Diamondbacks were on a road trip, which meant the whole block felt deserted.

Jack couldn't help but smirk.

Maggie shot him a look. "What?"

Jack shrugged. "You pick this place on purpose?"

Maggie arched a brow. "It's a good restaurant."

Jack huffed out a low chuckle. "Right next to a ballpark, huh?"

Maggie smirked. "If you don't like it, we can go somewhere else."

Jack shook his head, shoving his hands in his pockets as they crossed the street. "Nah. It's fine."

Maggie let that sit for a second, then—soft, teasing—"You miss it?"

Jack didn't answer right away.

He glanced at the stadium, at the empty concourse stretching under the streetlights. The place he used to belong.

Then he looked at Maggie.

And something in his chest settled.

"I don't know," he said finally.

Maggie didn't push. Just smirked, nudging his arm. "Come on.

Drinks first. Existential crisis later."

Jack chuckled. "Fair enough."

The restaurant was half-empty, warm and quiet.

Jack ordered a bourbon. Maggie got wine.

The waiter disappeared, leaving them in the kind of comfortable silence that wasn't really silent at all.

Jack leaned back, watching her.

Maggie arched a brow. "You're staring."

Jack didn't deny it.

He took a slow sip of bourbon, let the weight of the last few weeks settle between them.

"You know, I didn't expect to still be here," he admitted.

Maggie didn't blink. "I know."

Jack exhaled, tapping a finger against the rim of his glass. "And now?"

Maggie's lips curved slightly. "You tell me."

Jack smirked, shook his head. "You're impossible."

Maggie just took another sip of wine. "And yet, here you are."

Jack watched her for a long moment, the heat between them settling in like something familiar, something inevitable.

And then—

"Wanna get out of here?" Maggie asked, voice even.

Jack didn't hesitate.

Jack woke up to sunlight creeping in through the curtains and the sound of Maggie moving somewhere in the house.

He rolled onto his back, eyes landing on the ceiling, the kind of slow morning he hadn't had in years.

Then—the smell of coffee.

Jack smirked, pulling himself out of bed, stretching as he padded into the kitchen.

Maggie was leaning against the counter, already dressed, already sipping from her mug.

She looked up when she saw him. "Morning."

Jack smirked, voice still rough with sleep. "This where you tell me last night was a mistake?"

Maggie took another slow sip, eyes locked on his.

Then, finally, she said, "No."

Jack exhaled, rolling his shoulders. Good.

Maggie tilted her head, watching him. "You gonna stick around, Riggs? Or just crash at that kid's condo until he loses it in his divorce?"

Jack leaned against the counter, mirroring her stance. "I don't know."

Maggie arched a brow.

Jack smirked, reaching for the coffee pot. "Ask me tomorrow."

Maggie let out a quiet laugh, shaking her head. But she didn't look surprised.

She just sipped her coffee like she already knew the answer.

CHAPTER THIRTY EIGHT

Jack opened his laptop, not expecting much.

His inbox was usually the same—team emails he no longer received, the occasional check-in from an old player, junk he didn't care about.

But then he saw it.

From: Ryan Riggs

Subject: Big news

Jack straightened slightly, his fingers hovering over the keyboard before he clicked it open.

Dad,

Figured I should let you know—I'm being transferred to Luke Air Force Base (It's near Phoenix). Should be in there in a few months. I'll finish out my last stretch there.

A couple of the guys and I are looking into opening a gym in Chandler after we're out. Nothing huge, but a place where vets can train, maybe work with some local kids. Could be something real.

Anyway. Just thought you'd want to hear it that I'm leaving Iraq and out of the Army soon.

-Ryan

Jack exhaled slowly.

He read it twice.

Then a third time.

Luke Air Force Base. Then Chandler.

His son—the one he hadn't been able to reach for years, the one who had been a stranger more often than not—was about to be in the same damn city.

For the first time in longer than he could admit, Jack felt something settle in his chest.

It wasn't certainty, not yet.

But it was something.

And after all these years, that was more than enough.

CHAPTER THIRTY NINE

A week later, Maggie sat in her office at PFI, flipping through staffing requests and partnership proposals.

She felt settled here now. Like she wasn't just exposing something broken—she was fixing it.

A memo landed in her inbox.

Subject: Youth Baseball Program Needs Instructor

She scanned the details.

A local rec league was looking for an experienced coach. Someone who knew how to work with kids, how to teach fundamentals, how to keep them engaged.

Maggie smiled.

She dialed a number.

Maggie: "You busy?"

Jack: "Why?"

Maggie smirked, leaning back in her chair.

Maggie: "I think I found your next job."

29764692R00083